Lydia B

A CHANCE ENCOUNTER

AUSTIN MACAULEY PUBLISHERS™

LONDON • CAMBRIDGE • NEW YORK • SHARJAH

A CIP catalogue record for this title is available from the British Library.

ISBN 9781035831586 (Paperback)
ISBN 9781035831593 (ePub e-book)

www.austinmacauley.com

First Published 2024
Austin Macauley Publishers Ltd®
1 Canada Square
Canary Wharf
London
E14 5AA

Lydia Benham is a retired teacher of foreign languages; it has long been her ambition to write a novel. With her family background of Welsh/German parentage and an army upbringing, her novels reflect her love of languages, travel, skiing and music.

To my family, with love.

Chapter One

Luc was furious. He had just had to fire his long-term assistant and he was fuming! This was not a good time to be having to interview candidates. He was snowed under with work and besides, it took so long to train someone new. Why did the stupid woman have to go and complicate things? They had worked together for three years and things were going so well—then she had to go and spoil everything! He was so angry and frustrated—he just did not have the time for this.

Feeling like a caged lion, Luc angrily paced up and down in his studio. Damn, he couldn't concentrate on work. He knew he was being a coward, hiding in his basement studio while Camille packed her bags upstairs. They had said everything there was to say. He had given her an excellent severance bonus in lieu of notice and a good reference. She had no cause for complaint! She really was an excellent assistant. Luc would miss her efficiency. But he would not miss the added complications she had recently brought to his life. His overwhelming feeling was one of relief, despite the increased workload this would cause.

Luc felt that he had to get out or he really would go mad. Rushing upstairs, he quickly found his ski clothes. Down to the garage for his ski equipment and he was off!

Ten minutes later, Luc was in the cable car taking him right to the top of the mountain. Already, he was breathing more easily. Once on the slopes, he would be able to ski off his bad mood, and by the time he got back home, Camille would have gone.

The cable car clanked to a halt, decanting its passengers on the icy slopes of the glacier. Seasoned skiers they took no time at all to don their skis and start the steep descent. Luc was one of the first to set off not wanting to get caught up in the crowd. An advanced skier, he made quick progress, exhilaration pulsing through his bloodstream. He loved the adrenaline rush that he got every time he came up to the glacier. God, he needed this! He could feel his black mood lifting with every turn.

He was halfway down the mountain before he stopped to draw a breath. Usually, he would do the descent without a stop, but today, he wanted to draw a breath and just marvel at the scenery. How he loved these mountains, they were in his lifeblood. He was so lucky to live here!

Born in Geneva to a German father and a French mother, Luc had learnt to ski as a toddler. He adored his homeland and could not think of living anywhere else. Of course, he had spent time away—as a teenager studying music in Milan and Paris, but he always came home. As a child, he had also travelled widely with his parents as his mother was a famous opera singer. His father, a talented pianist, would accompany her on her tours, taking the young Luc with them accompanied by a nanny. When he grew older and his own musical talent was identified, he obtained a scholarship to both Paris and Milan.

Despite spending a lot of the year on tour, his parents always ensured that chunks of time were reserved for family time—especially Christmas and no bookings were ever accepted at this time, no matter how lucrative. So, Luc not only appreciated his home but also his family life.

Now a famous tenor himself, renowned throughout the world, he endeavoured to follow these same guidelines, keeping Christmas sacrosanct and always returning to his family home in Geneva where his parents were delighted to greet him. Luc could have chosen to live anywhere in the world but with the fortune he was fast amassing, he bought a luxurious gated house here in Gstaad and an apartment in Geneva.

He had designed the house to suit his needs. The basement housed a sound-proofed recording studio, an indoor gymnasium with swimming pool and sauna, a large garage for his various cars and a heated locker room for his ski equipment.

On the ground floor, the huge double front doors opened into a wide, elegant hallway. To one side an enormous modern kitchen extended the whole length of the house with wide bi-fold doors opening out onto a terrace. To the other side was an elegant lounge with three large comfortable sofas forming a seating area around a large wood burning fire. Plush cushions were piled in each corner, fluffy sheepskin rugs were scattered around the room and soft throws were carefully draped over the backs of each sofa. Soft lighting, shelving full of books and CDs and a sophisticated music system completed the look. It was a room designed for comfort and relaxation.

The top two floors housed four double bedrooms with their own ensuite bathrooms. Luc had selected the uppermost bedroom for his master suite as the views were stunning. With a dual aspect and French windows on both sides giving out onto balconies, Luc never tired of the magnificent view of the Swiss Alps. He could not envisage living anywhere more perfect and he was extremely grateful that his talent had allowed him to afford such luxury.

Perched halfway down the mountain counting his blessings Luc could feel his bad mood lifting. He was such a lucky man—he would not let Camille and her tantrums affect him this way.

With his good mood restored, Luc resumed skiing. The joy of travelling fast downhill could not be beaten, in his opinion. With just two weeks until Christmas, the slopes were getting busier with people taking extended holidays. The nursery slopes in particular were attracting the children's classes as schools finished for the holidays.

The only hindrance on the slopes were the novice skiers who were a danger to themselves and others with their out-of-control behaviour. Take that girl, for instance, who had just slipped off the T-bar lift and seemed unable to move out of the way of the oncoming skiers. *She was going to get crashed into if she didn't move,* he thought.

What the heck! Luc decided to go and rescue the fallen skier before she caused any damage. Coming to an abrupt halt alongside her, Luc reached down and hauled her to her feet, at the same time pushing her out of the way of the oncoming lift. He then bent to retrieve her poles and handed them to her before skiing off, his good deed done.

Angharad Morgan, known as Hari to her friends, was not enjoying her first attempt at skiing after a gap of ten years. She was frustrated to realise that she had forgotten everything she had ever learnt about the sport. Mind you, she had only ever had one week's experience when her parents paid for her to go on a school ski trip to the French Alps. She had really enjoyed it at the time and thought that she had skied rather well. Obviously not! Now, she could barely balance on the dratted things. Her hired boots were crippling her and her legs felt like jelly.

To top it all, she had just fallen off the T-bar lift on the nursery slope! How humiliating was that! Even the absolute beginners were doing better than her. Then to add to her humiliation, she could not move out of the way of the oncoming skiers as she had fallen onto her skis and dropped her poles. She had forgotten how difficult it was to push yourself up when on a slope. Thankfully, that stranger had hauled her to her feet and got her out of harm's way. Then he had skied off before she could even thank him.

Ah, well! She should just concentrate on getting down this one small nursery slope and maybe call it a day! After all, how difficult could it be?

Hari soon found out how difficult it proved to be. She made wobbly progress across the slope but was unable to execute the very simple snowplough turn as she approached the edge of the piste. Muttering instructions to herself, she pushed down heavily with both knees but her skis refused to turn! Hari did the only thing she could in the circumstances and fell over before she careered into the deep snow.

Damn! This was so frustrating! She was so annoyed with herself. Why couldn't she do a simple turn? Exhausted and demoralised, Hari breathed deeply wondering how she was going to get out of this mess.

Meanwhile, Luc had been having misgivings about not checking whether the young girl had managed to extricate herself from her predicament. He reasoned to himself that it was not his job to worry about lone beginner skiers but there was a vulnerability about her that touched him. So, against his better judgement, he took a chair lift to the intermediary stage and skied back down to check on the girl. He was glad that he had followed his instinct when he watched her careering wildly towards the edge of the piste, muttering, 'turn, damn you!' to herself as she failed to execute a simple snowplough turn and tumbled into the deep snow. He almost laughed at her dilemma but really what on earth did she think she was doing on a ski slope? She had no idea at all!

With a sigh, Luc once again skied alongside the girl and hauled her ungraciously to her feet. He retrieved her poles and literally turned her round so she was facing the other direction. She was so startled by his appearance that she forgot to turn her skis across the slope and before they both knew what was happening, she was careering downhill fast! With a scream of fear, she once again made herself fall over. This time her skis released under the pressure of the fall and disappeared down the slope.

Unbelievable, Luc cursed under his breath, as he went to rescue her for the third time! He skied down to retrieve her skis and poles and then side stepped back up the slope to the prone figure. Pulling her upright, Luc asked her in English if she was hurt as he had overheard her earlier mutterings and realised that she was probably a tourist—as if her level of skiing had not given that away! Hari muttered sullenly that she was fine, though feeling anything but! How on earth was she going to get down off this slope? Was this guy actually laughing at her? How dare he! She could feel her temper building both with the frustration at being unable to do even basic skiing and at this strangers repeated rescue attempts. How humiliating! And he seemed to be enjoying her discomfort! She was having difficulty controlling her temper!

Once her skis had been restored to her for the third time, Hari was desperate to get away from this smiling stranger. Foolishly, she pushed off in too much of a hurry and only succeeded in skiing right into him, taking him completely by surprise and knocking him over. Luc landed uncomfortably on his back—something that had never happened to him on the slopes! Even worse, a small body landed on top of him.

A startled pair of green eyes was peering at him through misted up goggles. Was that really gorgeous red hair creeping free of the helmet? Suddenly finding the situation extremely funny, Luc put his arms around the little body. Oh ho! Feminine curves! So she was not the little girl he thought she was at first glance. Without realising what he was doing, Luc impulsively kissed the plump lips in front of him. It was as if he had been struck by a bolt of lightning. She must have felt it too as her eyes widened with shock.

"Oh, you arrogant pig!" she shrieked and pushed herself off him. "How dare you!"

"Oh, come on, it's only a bit of fun!" Luc protested. "Here, let me help you up!"

"Don't bother! I can manage!"

She had a charming accent which Luc could not quite place. He was intrigued by her. She was very petite, so small in fact that he literally took her to be a teenager. But he had felt some luscious curves under those horribly baggy clothes and those eyes? Wow! She also had a temper from the glowering looks she was throwing at him. Luc could feel his interest piqued. He was determined to find out more about her.

Ignoring her protests, Luc got them both back on their skis and taking the initiative he deliberately positioned her between his own skis so that her body was resting against his own and proceeded to slowly ski them both down the slope. Angry at his presumption—how dare he treat her like a child! Nevertheless, Hari was relieved to be safely down and back on level ground. She knew she was beaten and was humiliated by her poor showing.

She was even more incensed to realise that the stranger had skied them down to the restaurant and was releasing both their skis. How dare he? Well, she was not going to stay here and socialise. Before she could protest, he had stacked both their skis and poles and was gently ushering Hari to a table on the terrace.

"Sit there, I will be back directly," he ordered.

Although angry at his high-handed attitude, Hari was too shaken to move. She took off her helmet and goggles and the stifling oversized jacket. Gosh, she must look a sight! She would just get her breath back and then leave.

Chapter Two

Luc returned with two mugs of hot chocolate and two slices of Apfelkuchen topped with cream. He felt she needed the sugar after all that energy expended from falling over. He caught his breath when he saw the lady facing him. Gone was the oversized padded jacket, helmet and goggles to reveal a rather gorgeous red-head. Those eyes! Wow! They were magnificent, like emeralds! Oh no! She did not look happy!

He smiled at her charmingly offering her the cake and hot chocolate. He was convinced that she was going to refuse them but then she obviously thought better of it. Muttering an ungracious thanks, she tucked into the cake, refusing to look at Luc. Gosh, she was hilarious! Luc was surprised to find that he was enjoying himself. The day was certainly turning out better than it started.

"So, I take it that you are new to skiing?" He asked innocently. "What brings you to Gstaad?"

"I work here," she grumbled, "not that it is any of your business. Just because you helped me does not give you the right to ask questions!"

"I rescued you three times," he protested with a smile. "So, as a reward, tell me a little about yourself. Then you are free to go and we need never meet again!" Seeing that she had made quick work of her cake, he pushed his own plate towards her, saying that her need was greater than his. Hari finally looked up and was shocked to realise that with his helmet and goggles removed, there was a very handsome man facing her! Oh my! That made her humiliation even worse. He looked so cool and relaxed, wavy blond hair and the coolest blue eyes she had ever seen. This was so embarrassing! And he had kissed her!

Trying to maintain her composure, Hari blushed at the memory, then took a deep breath and introduced herself.

"My name is Angharad Morgan, but my friends call me Hari. I am currently working for an English couple as an au pair to their four-year-old daughter. She is in kiddy ski school and I am to collect her at midday."

"That is a lovely accent! Not English though?"

"No, I am Welsh. My family lives in the Rhonda Valley, in South Wales."

"But I thought the Welsh were small and dark haired?" Luc exclaimed.

"Where do you get your colouring from?"

"From my Irish grandmother."

Deciding that she had given quite enough information away to this total stranger, Hari quickly finished her drink and got up to leave.

"Well, thank you for rescuing me and for this. Can I pay my share?"

"Certainly not! It is my pleasure!" replied Luc, sorry to see this intriguing lady go. He would get himself another drink and observe her movements from this terrace which overlooked the ski school.

Hari quickly gathered up her belongings and went to fetch her skis and poles. Her legs were sore and shaky as she made her way over to the ski school meeting place. She was relieved to reach the lockers so that she could lock away the offending ski equipment and replace the hideously uncomfortable ski boots with her soft, cushioned moon boots. Oh, that was sheer bliss! The foam interiors comforted her poor blistered feet. At this point in time, Hari never wanted to put on ski boots again.

She was early for meeting Amelia, but she could not have sat facing that smug stranger a moment longer. Hari realised that she did not even know his name. Well, it did not matter as she never intended to see him again. He had certainly got under her skin. She kept remembering that kiss. Despite all her denials, it had affected her. There was a definite frisson between them and this made her angry!

Reliving her encounter with Luc only served to increase Hari's discomfort, so she was relieved to see the children's ski class returning to base. There was Amelia looking forlorn—bless her! Probably had as fun a morning as her own! Rushing towards her, Hari quickly unclipped Amelia's miniature skis and picked the little girl up for a cuddle.

"Hello, Cariad, give me a cwtch!" she said comfortingly. "Did you have a good lesson?"

"Nooooo! I fell over!" sobbed Amelia, giving Hari a tight cuddle.

"Did you, Cariad? Well, I can beat that! I fell over four times!"

"You never!" replied Amelia, wide eyed and startled out of sobbing.

When Hari nodded, smiling into her eyes, Amelia gurgled, "Oh, Hari, you are silly!"

"I know, Cariad, that's why you like me, isn't it?" She asked, tickling the little girl into submission. "Come on, let's get those boots off and get you home. Shall we have eggy bread for lunch?" She asked, knowing this was Amelia's favourite. The little girl nodded happily, restored to her usual good humour, the skiing lesson quite forgotten.

Luc watched all this from the terrace quite enchanted with how Hari had coaxed the little girl out of her crying. She was obviously good with children. He wondered who the English family were that she worked for. Would he see her again? He hoped so, as she had got under his skin. He could still feel the after-shock of that kiss and wondered if it was a one off. He surely would like to find out!

When Hari got back to the house with a really tired Amelia, she found her employer already in the kitchen. Amelia's mother, Elizabeth Acaster-Wilkes was newly pregnant with her second child and not enjoying this nauseous stage. She had not enjoyed her first pregnancy and had no reason to suppose that this one would be any better. Her husband, Charles, dismissed her queasiness and moods and refused to allow anything to interfere with his social life. He was determined to enjoy this month skiing and socialising and was annoyed with Elizabeth for spoiling things with being off-colour.

Hari liked Elizabeth as much as she disliked Charles. If it were not for Elizabeth and the lovely Amelia, she would have resigned immediately. Charles was one of those men who made her feel uncomfortable. He always seemed to be in her way, was too touchy-feely and seemed to undress her with his eyes. He made her cringe to be near him and she tried hard not to be left alone with him. Unsure whether Elizabeth was aware of her husband's lecherous behaviour, Hari did not want to be the one to draw her attention to it, especially not when she was in a delicate condition.

"Hi, Hari! Amelia! Did you girls have a good time?" Elizabeth asked.

"No, Mummy! I fell over!" said Amelia sadly.

"Did you, precious? Come and give your mumma a cuddle! Did you hurt yourself?"

Amelia nodded and cuddled against her mother; she stuck her thumb in her mouth. She looked so tired that Hari wondered whether a nap might be in order. "Shall I make us a little snack?" She asked Elizabeth.

"Then I think, this little lady might need a nap."

"Yes, please, Hari. Then Amelia can have a nap with me. I feel like a rest, too. Would you mind fetching a dress for me from the dry cleaner this afternoon?"

"Not at all, I wouldn't mind a little look around and the walk will do me good as my legs haven't recovered from the skiing."

"Oh, did it not go well?"

"I was appalling! I spent more time on the ground than I did upright," laughed Hari, reluctant to tell Elizabeth about her good-looking rescuer.

"Oh, Hari. I am sorry I thought you could ski already. Maybe we should pay for lessons for you, too."

"The way I feel at the moment, I never want to get on skis again!" she replied.

After lunch, Elizabeth took Amelia to her room for a sleep. Hari went up to her own room to shower and change into something more comfortable and more flattering. She must have looked a real fright in Elizabeth's old ski suit as there was a six-inch difference in their heights and the suit was bought when Elizabeth was still carrying a lot of post baby weight. It drowned Hari! No wonder, Luc took her to be an overweight teenager! Hari did not know why this notion bothered her, but it did!

Feeling much more like herself, dressed in slim fitting jeans and an emerald green polo necked sweater, Hari added her moon boots, her favourite bronze-coloured puffer jacket and her cream bobble hat. Snug and warm she set off to run her errands.

It was a beautiful afternoon and Hari found herself enjoying the short walk into the town centre. Fortunately, she loved window shopping because she would not have been able to afford the expensive goods sold in this rather exclusive resort. Until her divorce settlement came through, Hari would have to be careful with her money. Her husband, Rhodri, was being petty and refusing to agree to certain reasonable demands, not wanting the divorce himself. Hari was almost prepared to agree to anything just to see the back of him but he was at fault, he would not suffer financially with his army salary and the resulting pension. She had to be sensible and listen to her solicitor's sage advice.

Hari had met Rhodri, while at the University of Cardiff. She was studying languages and he was doing engineering. They dated on and off throughout their time there. When Hari returned for her fourth and final year, Rhodri went to Sandhurst to do his military training. They continued to see each other whenever possible, Hari being introduced as his partner at the various balls and social events. At his passing out parade, Rhodri proposed and then pressurised a more reluctant Hari into an early marriage with an overseas posting on the horizon.

Hari should have realised that Rhodri would never change. A charmer, and extremely good looking, he lived to flirt. He constantly assured a dispirited Hari that it was all harmless fun and she had nothing to worry about, but she knew he was lying. He simply could not be faithful to one woman. Catching him in their own bed with a close friend was the final straw and Hari packed her bags and left. His pride wounded Rhodri was being difficult about the divorce which he did not want. They were at an impasse and Hari was struggling financially having given up her teaching career.

Being a naturally optimistic person, Hari tried not to dwell on the past. She had a nice job; she was in a lovely resort and once she got her divorce settlement, she could think about her future. For now, she was happy and in control of her own life. That felt good!

She walked down one side of the town before crossing the busy road and then walking down the other side. She looked in each shop window, making a mental note of possible treats if she ever managed to save enough money. Elizabeth was a generous employer and often gave Hari little gifts of hardly worn clothes, perfumes and books that she had read and no longer wanted.

The sun was going down and it was turning noticeably cooler as Hari made her way to the dry cleaners to collect Elizabeth's dress. There was a grand ball at the weekend which Charles and Elizabeth were due to attend and this was to be her outfit. Hari hoped it would still fit her as Elizabeth was showing her baby bump and was eating more than usual to counteract the attacks of nausea.

The next few days passed uneventfully. Hari and Amelia both shunned further ski lessons, preferring to spend their time quietly at home. Amelia was an easy child to entertain, eager to join in all activities. They baked cakes and biscuits, they drew and coloured pictures and played games, Hari made simple sock toys but mostly they enjoyed reading together. At Elizabeth's suggestion, Hari had also started teaching Amelia basic French and reading simple picture stories in the language.

Elizabeth's sickness showed no signs of abating and by Friday evening, she was having doubts about being able to attend the Charity Ball. Charles was furious as he had to be there and he refused to go without an escort. He had an image to keep up, after all. He was a very wealthy businessman and these occasions were vital for promoting his companies and for networking. As his wife, Elizabeth had a duty to be there.

Saturday dawned and Elizabeth could not get out of bed. She was crying in distress as Charles took out his displeasure in petty ways. In desperation, Elizabeth begged Hari to deputise for her.

"Oh, no!" cried an appalled Hari. "I couldn't! I have nothing to wear. I wouldn't know what to say or do!"

"Don't be silly, Hari. You are used to such events—you told me about the balls you used to attend at Sandhurst. They don't get more formal than that!"

"Yes, but that's different," argued Hari.

"Not really," countered Elizabeth. "You would be doing me a real favour, Hari. I would make it worth your while. I will make sure that Charles pays you double time and gives you a decent bonus on top. After all, he can afford it. Please say yes!"

"But, even if he agreed, what should I wear?"

"Oh, Hari, I have wardrobes full of dresses I never wear. I am sure we can find something suitable. I have too many shoes, bags, etc. I could open a shop. It will be fun kitting you out. Amelia could help. We could have a fun girl's afternoon. I will even style your hair for you—I used to be good at that! Please, Hari!"

"Well, ask Charles what he thinks first," said Hari, weakening. Part of her was thrilled at the thought of dressing up, it had been so long since she had such an opportunity. But the downfall was that she would be on a date with Charles!

When Charles was consulted, he pretended to be outraged at the idea, giving Elizabeth a hard time. He was secretly delighted to be taking the gorgeous Angharad Morgan on a date! When he broached the idea with Hari, he was shocked at how many conditions she laid down before she would accept. Just who did the little madam think she was? After all, he was her employer! He found himself agreeing not only to double pay, and a huge bonus, but to a certain code of behaviour! Simply outrageous! Well, he would say anything to get his way and then they would see!

So, the afternoon was spent in Elizabeth's room. Hordes of dresses were tipped all over the place. Elizabeth and Amelia sat on the bed, propped against the pillows, providing a running commentary as Hari tried on dress after dress. Finally, it was narrowed down to three favourites; a gold halter neck, a sapphire blue off the shoulder number and a deep red strappy one. Hari dismissed the blue as being too revealing. She could not decide between the other two so it all came down to accessories. The advantage of the red dress was the fitted bustier. It was also fuller in the body which Hari felt more comfortable with. High heeled gold strappy sandals and a matching clutch bag, with a gold velvet shawl completed the outfit. Hari had to admit it looked lovely and fitted quite well.

Elizabeth ushered Hari off to have a long luxurious soak while she and Amelia had their nap. Then they would do her nails, hair and makeup. Despite everything, Hari was enjoying herself enormously. What woman did not enjoy being pampered like this? She was actually looking forward to the Ball.

When Charles appeared suitably attired in his black dinner jacket with red cummerbund and bowtie—which coincidentally matched Hari's dress perfectly! He was astounded at the vision in front of him. Hari was unrecognisable. Four-inch heels brought her up to his shoulder. The red dress looked magnificent on her—it had never looked that good on his wife! Her hair was resplendent—those gorgeous red curls tumbled down her back, with the sides clipped with diamanté slides. Matching dangly ear-rings, a necklace and bracelets completed the ensemble. She was stunning! Every man would be envious of him! He would make sure to enjoy every minute—after all, it was costing him enough!

Chapter Three

Charles looked every inch the millionaire businessman as he pulled up at the venue in his gleaming red Porsche. Handing over his keys to the car valets, Charles escorted a wide-eyed Hari up the grand staircase to the ballroom. Her eyes looked amazing—they literally glittered and those lashes! He could not stop staring at her! Who would have thought that this stunning red-head was his date for the night?

Apart from Charles' obvious interest in her and his lecherous looks, Hari was enjoying herself. She knew she should be feeling nervous but she had decided that as she was standing in for Elizabeth she should act the part! As Charles greeted acquaintances introducing Hari as a friend deputising for his poorly wife, he glowed with pride at the envious glances thrown his way. Hari smiled politely and enjoyed the obvious admiration in some of the men's eyes. Before long, she was being asked to dance from all sides. Charles, however, kept her hand firmly on his arm and stated that the lady had promised him the first dance.

But Charles was in no hurry to take to the dance floor. He wanted to circulate and show off his date. Taking two glasses of champagne from a passing waiter, he handed one to Hari. Protesting that she did not drink and would prefer an orange juice Charles insisted she have just one little glass—after all, it was a celebration.

There was to be an auction of promises towards the end of the evening and big money would be spent. Charles rashly promised Hari that she could choose something to bid for, money no object!

Too many men had approached Hari inviting her to dance, so Charles took her by the arm and pulled her towards the dance floor. He proceeded to pull her against him, in far too close an embrace, and led her around the floor. Hari felt stifled and try as she might she could not pull free. When the dance ended, Hari pleaded the need for the rest room and hurriedly escaped. As he left the dance floor, she caught the eye of a tall, good looking blond gentleman. *Who was that?* thought Luc. She looks vaguely familiar. What a stunner! That gorgeous red hair! Surely, that is not the scruffy Welsh girl he rescued on the ski slopes? He followed her progress with his eyes determining to check her out.

When Hari returned from the ladies, she was waylaid by an impatient Charles. He grabbed her by the arm and pulled her into an embrace.

"Stop it! You promised you would behave!"

"That was before I saw you dressed like this!" he replied. "You are a real temptress, so how can I resist you?"

With that, he proceeded to kiss her passionately on the lips. Hari pushed against him with all her might—God, he was repulsive! His hands were everywhere! She kept her lips tightly shut so that he could not use his tongue. Suddenly, she felt him being pulled off her. A tall blond man was informing Charles that he was promised the next dance. Before she knew what was happening, Hari was being led onto the dance floor and was in the arms of an extraordinarily good-looking man, who looked vaguely familiar.

"So, Miss Angharad Morgan, we meet again!" vivid blue eyes gazed deeply into hers. "I nearly didn't recognise you in your finery! What a difference—you look stunning!"

"Thank you, I think," replied Hari. "Have we been properly introduced?"

"My name is Luc Wenger. Very pleased to meet you! May I call you Hari?"

"Are we friends, then?"

"I should think so! After all, I rescued you three times! Four, if you count just now. Who is that oily individual you were in the clutches of?"

'That, unfortunately, is my employer. Charles Acaster-Wilkes, millionaire and insufferable bore. He thinks his money will buy him anything!'

"Why are you here with him? Forgive me but he does not seem your type?"

"How would you know what my type is? If you must know, his wife is pregnant and suffering a lot of all-day sickness. She begged me to deputise for her as this is an important event for her husband. They bribed me with double pay, a huge bonus and he promised to behave like a gentleman. I could hardly refuse. How was I to know that his definition of a gentleman is no way near mine? I am hoping to slip away but he won't let me out of his sight. He even stalked me outside the ladies!"

"And if I were to rescue you? What would you say?"

"Don't even think about bribery! I have had enough of that for one night. Thank you for the dance. It was nice to meet you Mr Wenger."

With that, Hari walked off the dance floor straight into Charles who had been hovering nearby, watching jealously from the side lines.

"Who was that man?" He blustered. "How do you know him?"

"I have never met him before," Hari replied. "Not that it is any concern of yours! Now, if you don't keep your hands to yourself, I shall leave and you can make your own excuses to Elizabeth. You should be ashamed of yourself especially since you promised to behave like a gentleman!"

"Oh, don't be such a party pooper, Hari! It is just a little kiss!"

"But an unwanted one. You know how I feel about this— I made my position quite clear before agreeing to come tonight. I knew I shouldn't have trusted you! Now, let's circulate but keep your hands to yourself. If I am asked to dance, remember I am a free agent, not your wife!"

With that, Hari stormed forward towards the ballroom. She was immediately approached by a good-looking man who asked her to dance. With a smile, she readily agreed, leaving behind a blustering Charles. Several dances later and Hari was still being sought after by dance partners and Charles was growing increasingly incensed. How dare she flaunt herself like that! She was his date for the night and she had spent so little time with him. He was drinking far too much and becoming quite belligerent. Time he took a stand!

As the dance ended, Charles pushed his way forward and barged other claimants out of the way.

"My dance, I think!" he protested grabbing Hari none too gently by the arm, and pulling her tightly against him.

"Charles, let me go! You are hurting me!" she exclaimed. But Charles was deaf to all protests—he only knew that she was his date and it was his right to dance with her. After all, he was paying her enough!

Hari was completely incensed at his treatment of her. Not wanting to cause a scene, she fixed a smile on her face keeping it averted from Charles boozy breath. How much had he been drinking? Honestly, he said he was here to network but seemed to be making no effort to charm people. He was like a man obsessed and she found it worrying.

"It is far too hot in here, let's get some fresh air," Charles was saying as he manoeuvred Angharad towards the balcony, despite her protests. Once outside, he backed her against the wall and grabbing her tightly, he proceeded to kiss her rather roughly. Angharad tried to push him away but he was too strong. "Why can't you be nice to me? You smile and flirt with all those other men but treat me so badly. I am paying you a lot for this date; you should be more obliging!"

"How dare you! I am not that sort of woman. Besides none of those men mauled me like you!" she remonstrated with him. "Now let me go!"

Instead of releasing her Charles increased his hold while trying to fondle her breasts. Wriggling to get free, Angharad felt the material rip. She was livid but unable to move. Suddenly, the pressure on her was lifted as Charles was forcibly yanked off her.

Of course, it was her rescuer again! Pleased as she was to be free of Charles' clutches, she could have wished for a different Sir Galahad! She blushed to feel his gaze on her as she clutched the ripped dress to cover her modesty. "You again!" blustered Charles. "Who do you think you are? How dare you interfere in matters that don't concern you?"

"I think the little lady would disagree with that comment, don't you? I clearly heard her refusing your unwelcome advances. You are an obnoxious bully."

Turning to Hari, he offered to escort her back into the room.

Charles stepped in front of her and threatened, "If you go with this man, you are fired! Do you hear? Without references!"

Hari could not believe her ears. Shaking with emotion, she found herself being led back into the ballroom by a solicitous Luc who had draped his dinner jacket around her shoulders. With his arm around her shoulders to keep the jacket in place, he led her towards the ladies room.

"Do you need to freshen up? Maybe do some repairs to your dress! Or would you simply prefer to leave?"

"Could we leave, please? I couldn't face that dreadful man again."

"Come, I will see you safely home," said Luc.

"Oh, please don't leave on my account!" replied Hari. "I am really grateful for your help but you don't need to come with me. I will get a taxi."

"No gentleman would leave a lady in distress like this," countered Luc. "I insist on ensuring that you are safely away from that awful man."

Waiting just inside the entrance, Luc summoned his car. While they were waiting, he turned to look at Hari who had momentarily stepped out of her shoes to rest her aching feet and he burst out laughing. She glared at him in astonishment—what was there to laugh at!

"Oh, I am sorry!" spluttered Luc trying to control his laughter. "But you look so funny! Like a small child wearing her father's coat!"

"I'm glad I am a cause for amusement," Hari fired back at him, with her eyes flashing angrily.

"Oh, dear, no offence! You just look so charming like that!"

Just then Luc was informed that his car was ready for him. Without further ado, he gathered Hari into his arms and carried her out to the car, bowing politely at the amused gaze of the doorman who opened the door for them.

"What do you think you are doing? Put me down at once!" spluttered Hari. "Now, don't be silly! You could hardly walk out in bare feet. Besides, I didn't want the coat to slip and reveal your torn dress. After all, I have a reputation to maintain!" he quipped.

Oh, what an infuriating man! He was always wrong footing her. Why did he keep on turning up when she was at a disadvantage? Hari was too cross with men in general to realise how unfair she was being to Luc. Oh, he just had to drive a Porsche, too. What a poser! She really could find nothing nice to say about him, she was in such a rage.

Carefully handling Hari into his car, a substantial 4 x 4 which dwarfed her slight frame, Luc was amused to see her indignation. She really had quite a temper, to match that fiery hair. He would just let her smoulder a while. Having no idea where to take her Luc starting driving towards his home, awaiting further instructions.

"Where are you taking me?" Hari suddenly asked, jerking herself out of her indignation.

"Where would you like to go?" Luc responded with a smile. She really was an adorable confusion of emotions, he found her quite fascinating.

"Well, as you have just lost me my job, I have no place to go!" she blustered angrily.

"Now, that is not fair! All I did was rescue you from the unwelcome advances of a boorish idiot! I did not get you sacked!" remonstrated Luc.

"As good as! You kept on interfering!" Hari quickly replied, knowing how unreasonable she was being. But she was suddenly out of her depth. Where could she go? Was she really fired? What would Elizabeth say? Could she really carry on working for Charles anyway? But then she angrily realised how much money she was owed and made a snap decision.

"If you could just drive me to my employer's address, I will pack my bags and find a hotel for the night. Once I get paid, I should have enough money to pay for my fare home— although I don't know where that is at the moment."

Luc duly obliged and parked outside the Acaster-Wilkes' residence, saying, "Take your time! I will wait here and drive you to wherever you want to go. You are unlikely to get a taxi tonight. Don't worry, I shall be fine here."

Hari started to protest but thought better of it. She hurriedly let herself in to the house and rushed up to her room. Throwing Luc's jacket on to the bed, she hurriedly undressed and changed into her own clothes. Then pulling out her suitcase she hastily packed all her belongings, hoping not to wake Elizabeth or Amelia as she was not prepared to give explanations tonight.

Then as quietly as possible, she carried the heavy case downstairs. As she reached the front door, she realised she had left Luc's jacket on her bed. So leaving the case she ran back upstairs to retrieve it.

Meanwhile, Luc had put her case in the boot of his car and was waiting once again in the driver's seat.

It was very different Hari who climbed back into Luc's car. Gone was the stunning goddess in designer clothes and back was the adorable pint-sized cutie. She had so many facets to her that Luc found her utterly captivating, and wanted to get to know her better. Suddenly, he had an idea which might suit them both. "Well, now, since you believe that I just lost you your job, I feel honour bound to offer you another one. No, hear me out! I have a business proposition to put to you which might be mutually beneficial. I have just parted company with my long-term assistant at the most inconvenient time. My diary is overflowing and I really don't have the time to interview and train someone new—so, you would be doing me a big favour if you would consider taking on the job. It could be on a temporary basis to see if we suit each other. What do you say?"

"What sort of an assistant?" Hari asked begrudgingly.

"Mostly admin, I am a classical singer and have a diary full of upcoming concerts. I am also producing an album. My assistant handles all my diary commitments, theatre bookings, hotel accommodation, correspondence etc. It is a live in job. You would have your own suite of rooms and access to my private gym, plus the use of a car. The salary is generous and the right person gets to accompany me on tours. What do you think? Oh, can you speak any other languages?"

"It sounds interesting, but would I be living alone with you?" Hari asked worriedly.

"I have a cleaner and a gardener who come in to suit my needs. My cook recently retired and I haven't found a replacement yet. So, at present, we would be alone. But one thing I will ensure you from the outset—this will be a business relationship only. This is why I had to sack my current assistant—she wanted a more personal relationship and I never mix business with pleasure."

"Of course, well that's good! I am off men in general and not looking for a relationship," countered Hari. "Yes, I speak French and German, and also a little Italian. I studied languages at Cardiff, and taught in army schools for several years."

"May I ask why you left that career to become a nanny?"

"Personal circumstances!" Hari replied enigmatically, not wanting to be drawn on the subject. But then realising that this was by way of a job interview she felt she had to elaborate further.

"I am married to an army officer but we are currently divorcing. As I left him, his stupid male pride has been dented, so he is being difficult about the settlement, consequently my funds are limited at the moment. When I left the marriage, I took a cookery course thinking of a possible career change. Right now I am in a sort of limbo!"

"Sorry to hear about your marriage. I can understand how you are not interested in a relationship. That suits us both then. Your languages would be useful. You know, I think you might quite like the job, especially if you like to travel. What do you think?"

"It sounds interesting. You are sure there will be no pressure or hanky panky?"

Luc laughed out loud at this. What delightful terminology! She really was enchanting! They would have fun together, he felt sure.

"Most definitely not!" he assured her.

"Well, in that case, I accept! But on a temporary basis to see if we would suit," she added so quickly that Luc might have taken offence. He was delighted when she went on to add, "I will even take on the cooking for you, if you like, until you find a new cook that is."

"Excellent. That could be one of your first jobs—hiring a suitable cook. Until then I would be delighted for you to step into the role if you think you will have the time. I keep my assistant very busy on the whole…Right, let's get you settled. Tomorrow, I will bring you back here to sort out any outstanding wages. If you prefer, I will come on your behalf as I appreciate that you will not want to face Charles again!"

"Thank you, that is very thoughtful of you," replied Hari.

"I told you; I am a nice guy!" Luc winked at her and started the car with a huge smile on his face. Suddenly, life was looking up. Who would have thought that rescuing this novice skier would lead to this arrangement? Both his job vacancies filled in one go and a charming new assistant to brighten up his days. He had no doubt that Hari would be an interesting assistant, life would not be boring with her around!

Chapter Four

Hari could not believe the gated house that they approached. Why, it was a proper mansion! Who was this man to be able to own such a place? When he drove into the underground garage, Hari gazed around in wonder. There were three other cars parked there—one of which was for her personal use he had said! Like a sleepwalker, she followed Luc as he gave her a quick tour of his house. His own recording studio! A personal gymnasium and a swimming pool!

Upstairs was equally amazing. She literally danced around the kitchen; it was magnificent. Luc grinned at her enthusiasm; it was infectious! Hari found it hard to contain her enthusiasm as each new room was revealed. She could not believe that this was to be her new home, albeit temporary.

Finally, when Luc showed her own suite of rooms, she let out a whoop of delight and hurled herself onto the enormous bed.

"I can't believe this! Are you sure this is all mine? I feel I should be paying you for all this luxury."

"Don't worry, you will be earning your keep!" replied Luc grinning at her obvious delight. "Why don't I bring your suitcase up so you can settle in? Get an early night and we'll talk about work schedules tomorrow. Shall we meet for breakfast at 8.30—I usually do a workout and swim first thing. I will try not to disturb you if you need a lie in. My rooms are directly overhead on the top floor. Feel free to use the gymnasium and pool any time you like. Good night, Hari. Pleasant dreams and welcome to the team!"

Too emotionally exhausted to unpack, Hari took a quick shower to freshen up and fell into the hugely comfortable bed. Absolute bliss! She was not sure what had just happened today but she was feeling excited for the future. Even if this job only lasted six months, it would give her a good-sized nest egg. She only hoped that she could work amicably with Luc— so far, she felt that they had not got off to a good start. As she drifted off to sleep, Hari spared a brief thought for Elizabeth and Amelia—she would miss their company. Maybe they could keep in touch despite her fallout with Charles—she hoped so!

When Hari woke the next morning, she was momentarily disoriented not recognising her surroundings. Then realisation slowly dawned as she remembered both Luc's rescue and his subsequent job offer. Remembering her ungracious acceptance of his help on the ski slopes and his intervention at last night's ball, Hari felt herself blush with mortification. Why was he being so nice to her? She had been ungracious and positively rude at times. Her parents would be appalled at her bad manners. Then she remembered the kiss! What did that mean? Could she manage to work harmoniously with him and avoid any emotional involvement? He was an exceedingly good-looking man and wealthy, too. Enough to turn any girl's head. She would have to have her wits about her and maintain a strict professional behaviour with her new boss as this was a dream of a job and she did not want to mess it up.

Glancing at the bedside clock, Hari was surprised to note how late it was. No time to unpack now. She jumped out of bed, rifled through her case for some clothes and took a quick shower. Rushing downstairs, she found Luc already in the kitchen cooking breakfast and looking amazingly alert after such a late night.

"Morning!" he greeted her, "did you sleep well?"

"Yes, thanks. That's an amazingly comfortable bed. But did I dream about the job offer?"

"No," he laughed. "That was genuine. Not having second thoughts, are you?"

"Definitely not! I just hope you aren't! I hope you don't regret it, but I am a hard worker and I shall try not to let you down. I am really grateful for this opportunity, you know?"

"Look, as I said last night, you are doing me a favour. Now, sit down and let me make us some breakfast. Then let us get to know each other a little better before I tell you about the job in greater detail."

"Oh, you don't have to cook for me," interrupted Hari. "I should be doing that!"

"I am actually quite a good cook, and enjoy making the occasional meal but unfortunately my work schedule gives me little opportunity for that. So, please sit down and indulge me!"

Hari was amazed how comfortable she was beginning to feel in Luc's company. He really was a lovely man, how had she got him so wrong! He told her all about his parents and his early life, his scholarships in Paris and Milan and his subsequent career. Why had she not heard of him? He explained that he used his middle name Sebastien as his stage name to preserve his anonymity. To date, he had produced five albums all of which had gone to the top of the classical charts. He was now collaborating on a 'duets' album with other singers, attempting to cross over to 'pop era', a new genre for him. He had his own recording studio in the basement and would often invite fellow singers to stay so that they could work together. Luc went on to say that he had several concerts booked in the coming months. He would show Hari how to access the relevant files later that day. It was all logged on the computer and he was sure she would find it relatively easy. Then Luc asked Hari to tell him a little of her background. She explained that she grew up in Wales— one of three sisters, she being the youngest. She was 28 years old, born Angharad Price to Emlyn and Blodwen Price.

Her eldest sister, Cerys was 32 and married to Bryn—they had two little girls. Her middle sister, Gwyneth was 30 and married to Dai; they had two little boys. Hari, as her family and friends called her, grew up with her husband, Rhodri Morgan a close neighbour. They were friends all through school and went to Cardiff University together, she to study languages and Rhodri to study engineering. He was a few years older than her and they started dating seriously at university. On graduating, Rhodri went on to Sandhurst to become an army officer where Hari was his partner at the balls and social events. He proposed at his passing out parade and against her better judgement, he persuaded Hari into a speedy wedding as he was due to take an overseas posting. They started their married life in Germany where she taught in the army school at the base.

"May I ask why you left your husband? Or is that too personal?" Luc queried.

"Well, he was always a bit of a womaniser—had to flirt, didn't he? I could put up with that even if I never liked it—made me feel small, didn't it?" She smiled at her unintentional pun being only 5 foot 2 inches tall! Luc smiled back nodding in understanding but let her continue. "Then one day I came home early from work with a stinker of a headache, see, and found the shyster in bed with a friend! Our bed, mark you! That was the last straw. I packed my bags and left without listening to his excuses. I had enough of his lying and cheating. I am worth so much more than that!" she added defiantly.

"Where did you go?" Luc gently asked.

"I stayed with one of my colleagues for a while which was embarrassing as it was a close-knit community. She wasn't surprised at me leaving Rhodri, but at how long I had stayed. He had a reputation, see? Anyway, I worked my notice, found another job in the *Lady* magazine and the rest you know."

"It seems you have not had much luck with men—your present employer is not to be recommended, either."

"Which one?" She beamed cheekily at him.

Getting the joke, Luc joined in her laughter, before saying, "I promise to be the perfect gentleman. You can count on my friendship and support. I think we are going to get on well together, Hari, despite our shaky beginnings." He added with a twinkle.

Hari agreed, realising what a nice man he was turning out to be. Not at all the dictatorial bully she had labelled him after their earlier meetings. He had rescued her several times on the slopes despite her boorish behaviour and anyone else would have walked away on seeing her in the clutches of another man. Yet he had come to her aid again and did not expect gratitude. He was a decent man and it was a long time since Hari had met one of those. She really hoped this job would work out as she found herself liking Luc more on closer acquaintance. "And now your husband is being difficult about the divorce, you say?"

"Yes, he is being a real twat! Injured his ego, I have, see! No woman is allowed to walk away from him. Well, he chose the wrong girl if he wants a subservient doormat!"

"Even I can tell on our short acquaintance that you do not fit that description!" laughed Luc. "Have you always had a feisty temper?"

"I don't know what you mean," blustered Hari, in a huff, until she saw his smiling eyes and relented. "I can be quite a hot head, but I am working on more self-control. Some things just get me riled up and I blow!"

"Well, I shall try not to 'rile' you, as you say and hopefully, all will be calm."

Chapter Five

Having finished their breakfast and cleared away, Luc suggested that he show Hari where she would be working. Tucked away on the ground floor, at the back of a very elegant lounge was a cosy study/office. It was dominated by a beautiful writing desk that would have graced any nineteenth-century mansion. To its left stood a more functional computer table holding the very latest in technology; an up-to-date computer with printer and fax machine. On the right, stood a second more modern desk with a set of telephones. When Hari asked why so many, Luc replied that one was his private line and the other two were for business. His agent tended to call on the blue phone. He found it easier keeping things separate that way. Of course, he had his mobile phone for personal calls that number was only given to a few close friends and family.

He then proceeded to give Hari her own mobile phone which his previous assistant had left behind on his insistence. He took her over to the writing desk and showing her where to find the key he unlocked the central drawer to allocate his diary and contacts book. Everything in there was duplicated on the computer, with all files backed up, but he liked to have the paper copy to hand. It was only locked away after working hours and both travelled with him on tour. He showed Hari a beautiful burgundy leather briefcase which he said his assistant took with her whenever they were out of the office. It came with a laptop and the mobile phone he had just handed to Hari.

"So, you see, we are always up to date. I will show you where we keep all the various passwords and then later you can log on to the computer and start to become familiar with my work."

"Now, I would like to show you where I do most of my work."

So saying, Luc led Hari down to the basement. He first showed her the gymnasium and indoor swimming pool with sauna telling her that she must feel free to use it at any time. He then took her into the ski equipment room with its heated racks.

"One of the first things we must organise for you are some proper ski lessons. I shall be giving you a generous advance on your salary and you must buy yourself some decent ski clothes that actually fit or they won't be effective in the cold. Also some brand-new boots—it is impossible to ski if your feet hurt all the time. You might also want to buy some gym clothes and a swimsuit if you don't already have them."

Before Hari could even begin to object, Luc hustled her to his recording studio or his office as he called it. He pointed out the light bulb outside the door. "When the light is on, it means I am recording, so you can't come in. You have to wait until the light is switched off. It is all soundproofed, so you won't hear me and I can't hear anything outside of this room. If you need to contact me urgently, there is a buzzer upstairs in the office. When you press it, a light shows in here and if I can, I will get to the in-house phone. So, don't worry if you have to wait a while. Otherwise, I take regular breaks to relax my voice and take nourishment'." Opening the door, Luc led Hari inside the studio. She was amazed at all the technology. There was a big recording deck and several microphones. The walls were covered with posters of famous opera houses, singers and there were racks and racks of CDs.

"Wow, what a lovely room!" enthused Hari. "It's absolutely brilliant! I can't wait to hear your music. What are you working on now?"

"My agent is encouraging me to do a modern album but at the moment, I am working on a Duets album. I am getting to work with some really talented people—I love it."

"Ooh, that sounds fun! Anyone famous, who I would know?"

Luc went on to name three or four artists whom Hari instantly recognised. When he said they sometimes came to work at his own recording studio, she got all starry eyed. Amazing! She would actually get to meet some of these famous people. Seeing her enthusiasm, Luc grinned and said that she would have to get used to it as when they were on tour or doing concerts she would be mixing with all sorts of celebrities.

Hari was only just realising what an amazing job she had landed—she felt like a child in a toy store—all her Christmases were coming at once!

"Right," said Luc breaking into her reverie, "it's probably time for some lunch, then we need to go and collect you wages and that bonus you were promised before doing some shopping. Real work will start tomorrow. Oh, by the way, what are you doing for Christmas?"

"I would like to go home to Wales. I haven't seen my folks in a while and I know they worry about me. But I don't want to bump into Rhodri, it is too soon and too raw. So, it all depends on whether they have heard anything from him. I guess, I shall have to phone later to update them on my situation and see what I can find out. The trouble is that they are very fond of Rhodri and think I am being silly throwing away a good marriage. I haven't told them the whole truth as they are friends with his parents. If I am desperate, would you mind if I stayed here?"

"Certainly not! But I will be going home to Geneva to see my parents. I hate the thought of you being alone, so if you are stuck, please accept an open invitation to my parents—even if you only want to come for a few days. There is plenty of room. We start with a church service on Christmas Eve. Family only on Christmas Day and then friends on Boxing Day. It is fun and they would be delighted to include you!" replied Luc.

"Oh, that is really kind of you but I couldn't possibly! I hardly know you and I don't know your parents. It would be a huge imposition! But thank you for the offer."

"Well, think about it. It would certainly be preferable to being on your own in this strange house. Now then, what would you like for lunch?"

"Oh no, allow me. It is time I started pulling my weight," insisted Hari, as she opened the enormous double fridge and found just the ingredients she was looking for.

"Have you ever had Welsh Rarebit? No, well you are in for a treat, bach!" she said with a smile, moving efficiently around the kitchen. In no time at all, Luc was offered his first taste of Welsh magic. Watching this happy, smiling Welsh woman, move efficiently around his kitchen, Luc felt optimistic about his new assistant. He was sure they were going to get on well if he could only forget about that connection he felt when he kissed her. He knew he was attracted to her and that worried him since business and pleasure do not mix well as he had found to his cost. Well, he would make sure he kept his relationship with this lovely lady on a purely platonic footing, no matter how much his hormones were telling him different! And she could cook, too! A definite winner!

Hari was amazed at how comfortable she was starting to feel in Luc's company. He was so friendly and easy-going; how could she have ever thought him arrogant and overbearing? As long as she didn't look too deeply into those mesmerising blue eyes, which set her pulse racing, she would be fine. She just had to keep things relaxed and avoid getting too close to him. She most definitely should not think about that kiss which made her all hot and bothered. She could handle this!

"That was excellent, Hari!" exclaimed Luc on polishing off his Welsh rarebit. "I shall certainly look forward to more of your cooking. Now how about we meet downstairs in half an hour and we shall go and get your money. Do you think you should forewarn Elizabeth of your arrival?"

"Good idea! I was thinking I should ring her. She must be wondering what has happened to me. She has probably been ringing me but my phone is on charge. I will go and check."

When Hari retrieved her re-charged phone, she did in fact have several frantic messages from Elizabeth. Taking a deep breath, she texted her to see if she was alone and available for a chat—her phone rang immediately.

"My God, Hari! Where are you? What happened to you? Why was your dress ripped? You have given me such a fright! Charles still has not surfaced—he was so drunk; he booked a room at the venue. I have been going crazy with worry!"

"Oh, Elizabeth, I am so sorry. I thought Charles would have explained everything! I didn't realise that he had not come home. The long and the short of it is that he sacked me with immediate effect. To be honest, he had too much to drink—hence the ripped dress. Sorry he got a bit amorous!"

"The shit! I bet he did! Are you alright? Where are you? Of course, you are not sacked. You must come back at once!"

"I can't, Elizabeth, as much as I will miss you and Amelia, I can't work with Charles. He was obnoxious and offensive. But you mustn't worry as I have really landed on my feet. Do you remember that guy I told you about who rescued me on the slopes? Well, he intervened last night and feeling bad about me getting sacked he has offered me a job as his personal assistant."

"Oh, Hari! Are you sure he is reputable? What do you know about him? He could be anyone!"

"I know what you mean but, don't ask me why as we got off to a bad start, but I trust him. His assistant quit this week and he was going to advertise. So, as he said, this arrangement could be perfect for both of us. Anyway, we are doing a trial basis, to see if we suit each other."

"But where are you staying?"

"In his house—it is huge and I have my own suite! It has got everything, indoor pool, gymnasium, recording studio—oh! I forgot to mention he is some famous singer, though I have never heard of it," Hari rattled on. "Name's Sebastien or something."

"Oh, my God, Hari! He is famous. I am surprised you have not heard of him. He is up there with the likes of Pavarotti! He is quite a looker, too, if I remember. Taken the classical world by storm, apparently."

"Well, I never! I really must google him! Anyway, he is really nice. He is very insistent that this is a working relationship and the salary is amazing."

"If he is genuine, then you have really landed on your feet. I am delighted for you but I shall miss you."

"We can keep in touch! Listen, Luc wants to bring me over to yours so that I can collect anything owing. How do you feel about that? Especially with Charles not being there."

"Oh, please do come. I can easily transfer the money to your account. Amelia would love to see you and I can't wait to meet Luc/Sebastien. By the way, what is his name?"

"He is Luc Sebastien Wenger. He uses his middle name on stage as it gives him some anonymity."

"Right, can't wait to meet him! See you soon!"

Since she was on a roll, Hari decided to ring her parents and update them on her whereabouts. Her mother answered on the first ring and was delighted to hear from her youngest daughter, who had been on her mind a lot since giving them the startling news that she had left her husband. Mrs Price thought it was all a storm in a teacup, especially as her son-in-law had been constantly in touch assuring them that it was all a misunderstanding. He did not want a divorce and would do anything to get Hari back. Her parents were inclined to agree with his assessment of the situation, especially since his was the only version they had heard. With only Rhodri's version of events, as Hari had been particularly tight-lipped on why she had walked out on what appeared to be a perfect marriage, they thought it would probably sort itself out given time.

Hari always was a bit of a hot head and probably got the wrong end of the stick, she would come round after a calming off period they were sure. So, Hari's mum was pleased to hear from her errant daughter. Just in time to organise Christmas, which was always a huge family affair. Hari didn't need to know that the Prices and the Morgans had been plotting how to get the two love birds back together. What they needed was some quality time together—Rhodri even hinted that they were ready to start a family.

Magic!

So, it was a very chatty conversation with Mrs Price having no inkling as to the change in her daughter's circumstances. Not giving Hari much of an opportunity to update her on her recent job change, Mrs Price kept the conversation focused on the forthcoming family gathering. She did such a good job of not mentioning Rhodri that Hari became suspicious. This was not like her mother at all— something was not quite right! When she finally managed to get a word in, Hari decided to put a spoke in her mother's wheel to see if she could draw her out somewhat.

"Mam, listen! I have just started a new job—the other one wasn't working out—and I am afraid that I shall be working over Christmas."

"No, Cariad! You can't be doing that! It is home, you must come—we are all expecting you. I have told everyone you are coming, too!" her mother protested.

"Everyone, Mam. Who might that be? Not the Morgans, by any chance?"

"Well now, Cariad, you know we always spend Boxing Day with the Morgans. Just wouldn't be Christmas without them, now would it?"

"But, Mam, you must realise that I am the last person they would want to see!" exclaimed Hari.

"Now, now, Cariad. Don't get in a pother! They know this is only a blip in your marriage. Rhodri has assured us that you are getting back together—he even hinted that you want to start a family. Duw, there's lovely and about time, too, if you don't mind me saying. I could do with another grandchild! More to love, isn't it?"

Hari was furious. So, that was his game. She might have known from his stalling over the divorce that he had no intention of agreeing to one. A blip, indeed! She was tempted to tell her mother the truth but realised that she probably would not listen as she was so keen on Rhodri's version of events. Well, there would be no happy ever after for this marriage!

Hari adamantly blocked all her mother's attempts at persuasion—even her secret weapon—tears! She was so angry how everyone was going behind her back that it would be a long time before she went home. Certainly not before her divorce was final. Then they would take her seriously. What hurt the most was that they were prepared to take Rhodri's word over hers. But then she hadn't really given them any details, so she had laid the path open for him. The snake—how she hated his overbearing, arrogant male ego!

Absolutely shaking with rage, Hari quickly put an end to the phone call saying there was someone at the door. She threw the phone across the room and luckily it landed on the bed. Giving vent to her anger and frustration, Hari grabbed a pillow off the bed and proceeded to pummel the wall with it, squealing with frustration. She was so wrapped up in her anger that she did not hear Luc tap gently at her door. Hearing loud noises from within and fearing that Hari had hurt herself, he opened the door and peered in. What a sight met his eyes! His red-haired termagant of an assistant was pummelling the wall with a pillow and yelling in frustration. Goodness, what on earth had happened to put her into such a state?

"Hi, can I come in? Is it safe?" He enquired from the doorway. Hari turned suddenly and blushed scarlet. Oh no! Caught out in such childish behaviour—what must Luc think of her? He probably would not want to keep her on as his assistant now. That would be the final straw. What a horrible few months these had been!

Putting the battered pillow back on the bed, Hari tried to restore some order to her appearance. Her shirt had come untucked, her hair was wild and all over the place and she was red in the face. Squeaking in horror as she caught sight of herself in the mirror, she shot into the bathroom saying, "Give me a moment, will you?"

"Take all the time you need," said Luc reasonably. "Why don't I meet you downstairs at your convenience? No rush!"

A mortified Hari washed her hot face, combed her tangled curls as best as she could securing them into a high ponytail and straightened her clothes. She applied some subtle makeup to calm herself down and dabbed on some of her favourite perfume. Then with a deep breath, she made her way downstairs fully expecting to be given her marching orders for the second time in as many days. Hearing music coming from the lounge, Hari decided to tap on the door rather than just entering. Luc looked up to see an extremely worried and chastened Hari. Interesting! This was a side to her character he had not seen before. What on earth had happened to cause such a furious outburst and now this worried look?

"Are you alright, Hari?" He asked with concern.

"Oh, Luc, I am so sorry about my behaviour. It won't happen again! Please don't sack me!" Her words tumbled out in a rush.

"Sack you? Why would I want to sack you?" He asked in astonishment.

"Well, you can't want to work with the maniac you just witnessed!" she blurted out. "But I promise it won't happen again! I just had a nasty surprise; some upsetting news and I was so furious I took it out on the pillow!"

Luc burst out laughing. She looked so contrite and so innocent—she really had no idea just how adorable she was!

"Well, I am just glad I did not get in the way! I think I will install a punch ball in the gym for you. Looks like you might need it, Red!" he added laughingly. Hari eventually looked up and was surprised to meet his concerned gaze. He wasn't going to dismiss her after all! He was actually laughing at her antics, not horrified as she had imagined he would be. Her legs felt weak with relief and she sank gratefully down onto the nearest sofa.

Luc poured a cup of coffee and brought it across to her. Then sitting down next to her, he prompted, "So, do you want to tell me what upset you so much?"

Hari was instantly conscious of his presence seated so close to her. He was a tall man and in excellent shape with his daily exercise routine. She felt completely dwarfed by him. To try and hide her embarrassment, she quickly took a sip of coffee and keeping the cup in her hands she talked to it, to avoid looking at Luc. He was so close it was unsettling and she dare not look into those eyes. "It was my Mam, see!" she whispered. "I was all set to tell her about my new job and everything. Well, not everything—she does not need to know the circumstances of me losing my other job. But she would not listen. She kept going on and on about Christmas and it being all about family and friends that I just knew she had something up her sleeve. Anyway, I tricked her by saying I had to work for my new boss over Christmas, so would not be home. That's when I knew she had set me up!"

"Rhodri has been filling their heads with lies—saying we are not splitting up, that we are planning a family together, that I had got the wrong end of the stick. And they believe him! I can't believe it! Well, I can really. He always was a charmer, the rat! Sorry! Then I hung up and threw the phone across the room. Not your phone!" she added quickly gazing at him from under her eyelashes and seeing his raised eyebrows.

Meeting those deep blue eyes disconcerted her and she quickly glanced back at her coffee cup, all coherent thoughts gone. Why did he have to be so good looking? Why was he such a nice guy? Why did he have to sit so close to her? She tried to calm her breathing and hoped he hadn't noticed her discomfort.

She quickly put the cup down as her hands were shaking.

Poor, Hari! She really was upset by her husband's behaviour which was not surprising. What she needed now was reassurance that he would not let her down, too. Reaching out, he caught hold of her shaking hands and said reassuringly, "Well, I guess that means you are going to be our guest for Christmas. I must tell my parents—they will be delighted! I hope you are prepared to be royally spoilt! Now, come on, let's go and do some shopping and take your mind off your rather devious husband!"

Chapter Six

Once in the car, Hari updated Luc on her conversation with Elizabeth. He was pleased to hear that Charles was not home for Hari's sake although he rather relished having a word with that sleazy individual. He was glad to see that Hari had regained some of her equilibrium and he was determined to give her plenty of distractions to chase away that worried look.

Elizabeth and Amelia hurled themselves at Hari and hugged her tightly. Amelia wanted her to come home—why had she left? Did she not like her anymore?

Hari bent down to cuddle the little girl and assured her that they would always be friends but that she had got a new job.

Luc also knelt down next to Amelia, saying that he was sorry to have taken Hari away from her but that he really needed her to organise his life. But he promised Amelia that she could come and visit Hari at his home. She should bring her swimsuit as he had a big pool in the basement. Amelia's eyes widened in delight and she quickly forgot her sorrow at losing Hari. Standing up again, Luc then introduced himself to a charmed Elizabeth, who could easily see how Hari had been persuaded to work for him. She would herself if he had asked her!

Leading them into the lounge, Elizabeth organised coffee and cakes. While they chatted about generalities, she surreptitiously watched the interaction between Hari and her attractive new boss. There was definitely an attraction between them but they were both trying to hide it. At no time did the conversation turn towards her sacking by Charles or his appalling behaviour. Elizabeth had no misconceptions about her husband and knew that Hari was blameless. Although she would miss her, she appreciated that working for Luc was a dream job and that she would be foolish to turn it down. She was glad that things had turned out so well for her.

When they had finished their coffee, Elizabeth asked Hari to follow her into the study. She asked Amelia to show Luc her books—maybe he would like to read one with her?

"He is gorgeous, Hari!" she said, once they were alone. "You, lucky girl! I would work for him in a heartbeat! So, all's well that ends well, hey?"

"I am looking forward to this job—it sounds so exciting! And the pay and benefits are very generous, too!"

"Talking of which—let me transfer the money we owe you to your bank account. What are you doing for Christmas? Going home?"

When Hari explained Rhodri's behaviour, Elizabeth shared her outrage. She was pleased to hear that once again; Luc had come to her rescue and that Hari would not be alone. But she questioned herself whether this was the behaviour of an uninterested employer. She reckoned that he was smitten with this lovely Welsh woman. She only hoped that no more heartache was waiting for her friend. Hari and Luc took their leave promising to arrange a meet up for Amelia very soon. They then spent the rest of the afternoon doing a major shopping spree. Hari had never met a more patient man than Luc when it came to shopping. He waited patiently while she tried on ski suits, gave his opinion on presents that she bought for her family, he even helped choose a suitable swimsuit and tried hard to persuade Hari to buy a bikini! He encouraged her to buy herself a Christmas outfit. He promised that his parents were not overly formal but he agreed that a selection of clothes, both casual and more formal, would be useful as they might be invited to a few parties, optional of course.

Putting the numerous parcels in the car, Luc then insisted on taking Hari out to lunch. He was surprised how much he was enjoying himself as he usually hated shopping. Watching Hari's enthusiasm was catching and Luc realised that he wanted to buy his own presents this year, rather than relying on Camille who used to sort it all for him. Seeing how Hari deliberated over each present, matching them carefully to the recipient, he realised how impersonal his presents were and he felt ashamed of himself. Being busy really was no excuse as he was sure Hari would admonish him!

Excited by all her purchases, Hari kept up an enthusiastic conversation throughout lunch. She pulled a little notebook out of her bag and made lists of what she had already bought and for whom. Then she added the names of people whom she still had to buy for. She wrote continuously while eating, stopping occasionally to exclaim how good the food was! She suddenly stopped mid-sentence and pointed her pen at Luc.

"Your parents, Luc? Tell me about them—what are they like, what are their hobbies. I need to find the perfect present." She kept her pen poised and ready to make notes.

"Well, Vati, Dieter Wenger, is a classical pianist. He loves classical music but is also fond of opera and jazz. He reads a great deal and is fluent in German, French and English with a fair smattering of Italian. I am going to buy him a cashmere sweater this year in red! Don't ask me why—it just seems right! Maman, Virginie Duplessis, is an opera singer, who has sung all over the world. In her downtime, she loves doing embroidery. I tend to buy her perfume but I want to choose something more personal this year. Maybe you could help me?"

"Love to! What is her colouring? Does she have a favourite colour?"

"Well, she has my colouring—blonde hair, blue/grey eyes. She is tall and extremely elegant. Wait a minute, let me show you some pictures on my phone." Luc scrolled through his mobile and found photos of both his parents. His father, Dieter, was an older version of Luc. Tall, handsome with dark blonde wavy hair and similar blue/grey eyes. His mother, Virginie, was a tall, elegant woman with blonde hair and blue eyes. Hari could see where Luc got his good looks from.

"Why not buy your Mam a peacock blue top—either a blouse or a sweater? Then I can buy her a co-ordinating silk scarf. Similarly with your dad, I could buy him a nice cravat to coordinate with the sweater. I shall also bake some Welsh cakes which are a cross between a cookie, a scone and a pancake and some bara brith, which is a type of tea loaf and means speckled bread."

Hari made notes as she talked, an efficient little organiser. Luc was feeling optimistic about his new assistant and was pleased with her appointment. She was the full package, a good cook, an efficient organiser and excellent company, too.

"That's a great idea! Maman especially will enjoy exchanging recipes with you. She loves to cook but does not always get the time."

"Do you have any other relatives whom I should buy for? Who else is likely to be there?"

"Just the immediate family on Christmas Day. As I said, some close friends and neighbours will join us on Boxing Day—but no presents needed."

"Right then, eat up, bach, we have shopping to do! I must finish off my family so that I can post them tomorrow, now that I am not going to be there," ordered Hari with a twinkle in her eyes.

Three hours later, Luc was seriously flagging. He was amazed at Hari's stamina and determination. Yet despite his exhaustion, he could not remember a day when he had enjoyed himself so much. He had never realised how rewarding it was to buy personal presents for the people he loved. Hari was proving to be such a good companion. Luckily, she was so organised that they had completed practically all her lists. She had even bought wrapping paper, tape, gift tags and cards.

Back in the car on their way back to the house, Hari had nonchalantly informed Luc that he could help her parcel up the presents after dinner so that she could post them first thing tomorrow. Then she was at his disposal to start work. She was surprised to see his shoulders shaking as he tried to suppress an overwhelming urge to laugh.

"Are you okay, Luc?" She asked in all innocence.

"Yes, thanks, boss!" guffawed Luc, just realising how his life would never be the same with this irrepressible assistant. Was he ready for the shock?

Suddenly, Hari realised what she had said. Oh, my goodness, she had had so much fun shopping with Luc that she had completely forgotten that he was her boss! What must he think of her? Blushing with embarrassment, she stammered her apologies adding that she had not meant to be so controlling. Luc laughed all the harder. God, she was incredible!

Chapter Seven

Arriving back home, a contrite Hari thanked Luc profusely for such a lovely day. She helped carry in all the parcels and carefully asked where Luc would like her to put them. She was determined to remember her position as his employee.

She really did not want to lose this job.

Once all the shopping had been stored in the lounge, Hari rushed upstairs to freshen up, before going to the kitchen to prepare their evening meal. Luc was already putting on a pot of coffee, and he forestalled her saying:

"Why don't we order a takeaway tonight? You have had a really busy day and there are a lot of presents to wrap. It will take a few hours at the very least. So, what is your preference—pizza, curry, Chinese?"

"I really don't mind—you choose. In that case, do you mind if I make a start on those presents?" She asked politely.

Luc smiled to see a more subdued Hari, politely deferring to him after her earlier bossiness. He felt that she would not be able to sustain this subservient behaviour for long as she was a born organiser.

A short while later when Luc fetched a tray of coffee into the lounge, he found Hari sitting on the floor completely surrounded by parcels. She kept referring to her notebook and was ticking off names with each parcel wrapped and tagged.

"Right, I have ordered an Indian takeaway with all the works, so I hope you are hungry. Here, have a cup of coffee and then tell me how I can help."

"Oh, thanks, Luc! No, really there is no need. I am sure you have better things to do with your time," Hari protested.

"But I would like to help. Besides, I ought to wrap my parents' presents myself. It is time I took more responsibility rather than delegating everything." So, Hari got Luc to help her wrap her nieces' presents. She wrote the gift tags and cards and attached them carefully to each present. Then she did the same for her nephews. As she completed each family's presents, she put them to one side for parcelling, and ticked their names off her list.

In between helping Hari, Luc poured cups of coffee and put on some background music. Hearing the gate buzzer Luc checked the intercom—the food delivery had arrived! Releasing the gate, he went downstairs to pay for the meal.

Then he called out to Hari to join him in the kitchen.

"Do you fancy some wine?" He asked her as she helped to dish up the food. "If you would like some, I will join you, but I am a bit of a lightweight with alcohol, it goes straight to my head. So, I will only have half a glass please!"

After a companionable meal, Hari insisted on washing up before returning to her parcels. She was surprised but pleased when Luc insisted on helping her to the bitter end! Gradually, the pile of presents were wrapped and packaged, ready for posting the next day. Hari ticked off the last name and gave a whoop of joy!

"That was brilliant! Thanks ever so much, Luc. I could not have done that without you! I'm shattered! I think I will have a bath and an early night. What time do you want me to start tomorrow?"

"Shall we meet for breakfast at 8? Feel free to use the gym and pool, if you like. You won't disturb me! Sleep well!"

Up in her room, Hari realised that she was in real danger of falling for Luc. He was such an interesting man, so friendly and considerate, attractive too. Not at all the overbearing man she had first thought him to be.

Despite feeling tired after such a busy day, Hari could not sleep. Her mind would not switch off—too much had happened and she felt off balance. She was furious that Rhodri was trying to manipulate her and that he had her family hoodwinked. She was equally furious at Charles' bad behaviour. What was it about her that allowed men to treat her badly? Was it her size? Did she come across as defenceless?

But then, she thought about Luc and this theory did not work. He had been nothing but kindness itself, even if it was mixed with a certain arrogance at times. It was his kindness that was breaking down her defences—she almost preferred it when they were sparring with each other. He had made it quite clear that this had to be a working relationship, so he must never know how attracted she was to him.

After hours of tossing and turning, Hari knew she would never get to sleep. So, she decided to go for a swim. Quickly putting on her swimsuit, she covered up with a dressing gown and grabbed a big fluffy towel. In trying to be quiet, so as not to disturb Luc, she stubbed her toe against the door jamb and cursed silently, tears springing to her eyes with the pain. Once she had recovered, Hari limped downstairs and was relieved to reach the basement without further mishap. Switching on the lights, she used the dimmer switch for subdued lighting. A second switch piped low orchestral music. With such a lovely ambiance, Hari could feel herself relaxing. Placing her towel and robe on a nearby lounger, she did a shallow dive into the pool.

Half an hour of gentle swimming did much to alleviate the tension in Hari's body. She flipped onto her back and allowed herself to float with her eyes closed, the lovely music hypnotically washing over her. She could feel herself getting sleepy, so reluctantly climbed out of the pool. Laying her towel on the lounger and wrapping herself in the huge fluffy robe, Hari was too tired to return to her room. So, she stretched out on the lounger and drifted off to sleep lulled by the tranquil music.

When Luc arrived for his early morning workout, he was surprised to find the pool room lit up and music playing. Peeping his head around the door, he was astonished to find Hari fast asleep. Having no idea how long she had been there, he decided to let her sleep. Fortunately, the gym was well soundproofed, so she should be undisturbed. He wondered what had prevented her from sleeping—she should have been exhausted after such a hectic day.

After his usual hour's workout, Luc was undecided whether to have his daily swim—he didn't want to disturb Hari but equally he liked his routine. He decided to go ahead but to be as quiet as possible.

Hari woke with a start and could not work out where she was. As she slowly remembered her insomnia of the previous night, she realised that someone was swimming in the pool. Oh no! Was that Luc? How was she to leave unnoticed?

Maybe she should pretend to be asleep and wait until he left? He was swimming confidently and rhythmically, completely absorbed in the exercise. She must have made a movement because he suddenly looked at her and smiled. Oh no! He was getting out of the pool. Gosh! He was gorgeous, so tall and well built. Hari felt her insides melt at the sight. She could not stop staring at him—to cover her confusion she shot to her feet grabbing her towel and clutching it to her chest.

"Morning, Hari! How long have you been down here? Couldn't you sleep?"

"No! I tossed and turned for hours until I gave up and came down for a swim. It is so lovely in here with the soothing lights and music that it did the trick and I fell asleep! Luckily, not in the pool!"

"Well, I hope I didn't disturb you. I am afraid I am a bit of a stickler about my morning exercise routine."

"No, not at all. Time I was awake anyway. Well, I had better go and shower. Give me half an hour and I will get breakfast."

"No rush. I can make my own, you know!"

"No worries—I love cooking, so you will have to indulge me. See you later," she said and rushed out of the pool room. Being in proximity to his nearly naked and very well-formed body was making breathing difficult. She would have to get a grip if she were to conceal how very attractive she found him.

When Luc walked into the kitchen a short while later, he was met with the delicious aroma of a cooked breakfast and filter coffee. A place had been set for him and Hari was just waiting to plate up the food on his arrival.

"Morning, I have made you a full English after your energetic workout. Hope that is acceptable? I should have asked you what you like."

"That's great, thanks. But aren't you eating anything?" Luc asked.

"Oh I have already had my fruit and cereal, thanks. I don't like a big breakfast. Now, sit yourself down and tuck in."

Hari was determined to keep this relationship on a firm business footing, so she busied herself around the kitchen, checking on stores and making notes in her little book. She could not allow herself to relax and sit down to eat with Luc as it would seem much too intimate. She had to keep a firm distance or she would be lost and she really wanted this job.

When Luc had finished eating giving his compliments to the chef, Hari removed his dishes and quickly took care of them. She was so business-like and efficient that he wondered if he had offended her. Gone was the feeling of camaraderie from the day before. Luc found himself regretting that loss. But he had stipulated from the outset that this would be a working relationship so he shouldn't really complain.

With her notebook ready, Hari asked Luc what he would like to eat for lunch and dinner. She checked what his favourite meals were and suggested that they keep a wall chart calendar showing when he would be home or away and when he required feeding. That way, she could work out her weekly food shopping routine. She also intended to do some bulk cooking so that she could freeze individual meals for his convenience. She insisted that she was happy to do the cooking as well as the administration work, adding that she was happiest when she was busy. Luc agreed to her dual role but stated that she had to say if it became too much for her.

Hari asked Luc if he minded her going out to send her parcels. She wanted to get a wall chart and coloured stickers to organise herself. She would feel happier once she had a visual chart clearly indicating his whereabouts and meal requirements.

Luc insisted that she used one of his cars for her own personal use. He showed her where to find the various security codes to access the house and he gave her a bank card for his business account, insisting that she charge everything to that account. They would sort out her salary later on and he would arrange a transfer of funds.

He would spend the morning in his recording studio working on some of the new songs he would be releasing. He assured Hari that she should take as long as necessary and that he was quite capable of preparing himself lunch, so if she wanted to have lunch out there was no need to rush back.

Hari could not believe what a considerate employer he was proving to be. Surely, the job could not be this good, could it? That Camille was a fool to quit, in her opinion. Then she remembered that Camille had fallen for her boss and made the situation untenable. Though she could quite see how anyone could be smitten with the lovely Luc, she was determined that she would maintain a polite distance.

Chapter Eight

So, followed a period of calm routine. Hari set up her colour coded wall chart showing Luc's diary commitments. She was excited to see two tours booked for the New Year, especially since Luc hinted that she would be accompanying him. Then, there were several individual concerts, mostly within Europe—such as an Andre Rieu concert in Maastricht and another with Céline Dion in Geneva, Hari could hardly contain her excitement.

By now, she had spent a lot of time researching Luc/Sebastien on the internet. He had a sublime voice—how had she never heard of him before? Listening to him singing when alone in her room at night, she felt herself melt at the emotion he conveyed. Her heart ached when he sang of love and loss, the tears running freely down her face. When he harmonised with another male voice, she thought she had never heard anything so beautiful. This new album would be a definite winner—she couldn't wait to buy a copy.

She also researched his parents only to realise that they were equally famous. His mother's voice was a pure delight, smooth and deep like warm chocolate it resonated deep within one's soul. His father was a very talented pianist, too. Never had Hari enjoyed classical music so much. She was overawed by the sheer talent in his family and was slightly nervous about meeting them. She just hoped they would not be divas!

But then she remonstrated with herself Luc was down to earth himself so why should his parents be any different. Hari was especially pleased when Luc consulted her on what songs he should include on his new album. He had several definite bookings with fellow singers who were delighted to duet with him but he still had to find another six tracks. Hari said she would give it some serious thought and produce a list of her favourite songs for him to consider. She was excited to find out which tracks he already had lined up and with which singers. She could hardly contain her excitement when Luc told her that one of her favourite singers, Jason Greene, an American baritone who not only sang classical music but had also branched out into more popular music, would be coming to record a duet with him.

"What, here? He is coming here?" She gasped. "Oh my goodness, when?"

"Sometime in January—he will probably stay with us for a week or so. I will leave you to co-ordinate the arrangements with his agent."

"Oh, my gosh! I absolutely love his voice! This is so exciting! I can hardly wait!"

While enjoying her obvious enthusiasm, Luc could not help feeling a modicum of jealousy. He only hoped she would not find him irresistible when she actually met him. So, while Luc had meetings with his agent, and spent hours recording various songs for selection, Hari switched on her iPod and started listing her favourite songs for Luc to consider. By the end of the day, she had a list of twenty songs for him to listen to.

Hari had never been happier. She cooked delicious meals, baked cakes and biscuits, all the time relishing Luc's obvious enjoyment of her food. Mindful of her forthcoming sojourn with Luc's parents for Christmas, Hari also baked some bara brith, some Welsh cakes and lots of cookies. These would be her contribution to the Christmas feast. As she cooked in bulk, she managed to freeze and label many meals. While in the kitchen, she invariably had her iPod playing and would sing along quite tunefully. She had the inherent Welsh love of singing and had sung in a choir both at school and at chapel.

She also enjoyed working as Luc's assistant—the job was interesting and varied. She really enjoyed liaising with Luc's agent, Monike who had a good sense of humour as well as being excellent at her job. Getting on famously, the two ladies agreed to make a lunch date and get to know each other better. This was particularly pleasing for Hari as she knew so few people in Switzerland that she was eager to extend her group of friends. Even though Monike was based in Geneva as she pointed out, it was only an hour or so away and she would be delighted to offer Hari house room for a visit. In response to Hari's query as to whom she should approach on Luc's behalf to work on his album, Monike gave her a list of singers and their agents to contact.

As Luc's diary started to fill up, Hari was glad to have her wall chart on hand to avoid double bookings. Although she worked hard, there was still plenty of free time. Luc was a generous employer, allowing Hari time off whenever she asked for it, encouraging her to make new friends. He also arranged for her to have regular ski lessons and Hari was pleased to find that she was actually losing her fear of skiing and making real progress. She did not mind the odd evening alone when Luc had a dinner date or another engagement, but she preferred those evenings when he stayed at home and they played board games, watched movies together or just simply read books, comfortable in each other's company.

She had also never been fitter. With her daily morning swim, her regular ski lessons and the occasional workout in the gym, usually when Luc was not there, she felt good about herself. She especially enjoyed the few occasions when Luc had gone skiing with her—revelling in his praise at her obvious progress.

It was Luc who reminded Hari of her promise to invite Amelia on a visit. He was so busy in his recording studio that he thought it would do her good to have her little visitor. Amelia duly arrived—Elizabeth dropped her off before leaving for a hair appointment—promising to stay for a coffee on her return.

Amelia absolutely loved the house. She was amazed at Hari's room and enjoyed bouncing on the bed and practising forward rolls across its vast expanse. "Why, Hari you could fit ten people in this bed!" she said open mouthed.

"No, Cariad. Not that many! I sleep right down the middle and can play at snow angels without ever touching the sides. Have a go!" she said, showing Amelia how it was done. Much giggling followed.

"Now, why don't we go down to the kitchen and make some cookies for your Mam? Then we can have a swim!"

"Yay, this is so much fun! Can I live with you, Hari?"

"Oh, that would be lovely, Cariad! But your Mam would be so sad if you did. Best to visit often instead, come on, cookie time!"

In the kitchen, Hari switched on her iPod as she always cooked best with a musical accompaniment. There was much laughter and singing as well as cooking. Once the cookies were in the oven, Hari found a suitable song on her iPod so that she and Amelia could dance around while waiting for the cookies to brown. She chose 'I could have danced all night' from the King and I, so that she could waltz around the room with Amelia. It was a particular favourite of theirs! Bending down to take the little girl in hold, Hari twirled her around the room while singing along at the top of her voice. They loved the part when the music got faster and they had to twirl ever faster themselves. They were quite breathless when the song ended and they fell laughing onto the settee.

"Again, Hari! Please!" giggled Amelia.

"Cor, you are a glutton, madam!" Hari groaned with a smile in her eyes.

"Once more then, Cariad, as the cookies are not ready yet!"

Restarting the tune, they took up position and set off with much giggling and singing. They were making so much noise that neither of them noticed Luc standing in the doorway watching them with a huge grin on his face. Deciding he wanted part of the action, he tapped Hari on the shoulder saying, "Is this a gentleman's excuse me?"

She jumped in fright and then laughed when Luc picked Amelia up into his arms and took over as her partner. His deep rich voice boomed out the song in time with the tune and he made an excellent job of spinning the little girl around. She was in her element. When the music ended, he held onto her a little longer to ensure she wasn't too dizzy. Then he put her gently down.

"Oh, that was even better than Hari! You go faster!"

"Oi, that's not fair," said Hari. "Cheek! After all I have done for you, madam!" she added with a glare at Amelia that set her off laughing.

"Dance with Hari. Make her dizzy!" she insisted.

Luc raised an eyebrow at Hari who blushed and said, "Now, Cariad. Luc hasn't got time for this. He is busy working."

"Oh, I am sure I could manage just one more dance," he protested. "Or are you afraid, Mrs Morgan?"

"Certainly not! Right then, here goes!"

Restarting the music, Hari offered her arms to Luc in readiness for the dance. Taking her in a firm hold, he grinned into her eyes and started dancing at a bewildering speed all the while singing the tune.

"Come on, Hari, sing along!" he teased.

She was almost too breathless to comply, but would not be outdone by this vexatious man! They danced so fast that Hari had to literally cling on to Luc for fear of tripping up.

"You can always stand on my feet," he quipped.

When the music ended, Luc kept a tight hold of Hari to stop her from overbalancing. He could feel her rapid heartbeat through his palm against her back, her face was flushed and she was out of breath. Every pulse in his body was aware of her proximity—he had an overwhelming urge to kiss those pretty lips. Luckily, he was brought to his senses by Amelia's excited laughter as she lunged at them both, wrapping her arms around their legs.

"Oh, that was so funny!"

Just then, the timer on the cooker pinged. *Saved by the bell!* thought Hari, in danger of losing herself in Luc's arms. Why did he affect her so?

"Right then," she said, all business like once again. "Time for a drink and some cookies. Not too many now, Cariad, or you might sink in the pool!" she quipped.

"Why, Hari, are your cookies so heavy then?" Luc asked innocently. "Do you think I will be safe in the water? Maybe I better not eat one!"

Amelia guffawed at this. He was so funny, Hari's new boss. She liked him.

He was nice looking, too. Even Mummy said so!

Just then, the buzzer went on the gate. Taking Amelia over to the entry phone, she showed her the image of her mother's car at the gate. Telling her to press the button, they released the gate and Elizabeth drove to the front door. An excited Amelia was on the doorstep to greet her.

"Mummy, I had so much fun! I bounced on Hari's bed. Big enough for ten people it is! We did rolls and snow angels. Then we made cookies. Then we danced. And Luc danced too. With me and then with Hari. It was fun. Now, we are going to swim but Luc can't cos he will sink. He ate six cookies!"

Elizabeth smiled at her excited little daughter. She was obviously having an excellent time. Laughing Hari led her into the kitchen.

"Sit down, Elizabeth. We were just having a coffee break then I am taking Amelia for the promised swim. If you like, you can bring your drink downstairs and watch from the poolside. There are some lovely loungers there. Unless you have brought your swimsuit and would like to join us?"

74

"Oh I couldn't possibly ruin my lovely new hair! I shall be more than content to sit in a lounger and relax. I shall let you two mermaids have your fun!" she quipped, getting a giggle from her daughter who had bought her Little Mermaid swimsuit.

"Oh, Mummy, you are funny! Hari isn't a mermaid!" she giggled.

"What? Do you mean to say Hari doesn't have a Little Mermaid swimsuit, too? How disappointing! Ah, well, my lovely girl, you shall have to be the only mermaid!" replied her mother.

Down in the pool, Hari helped Amelia into her pretty little costume and sent her out to Elizabeth to put on her armbands. Then she quickly put on her own swimsuit—rather modest black number, chosen not to reveal too much cleavage in case her swimming sessions coincided with Luc's. So far, she had been fortuitous in avoiding him.

Helping Amelia into the water, she carefully supervised her attempts at swimming. With regular practice, she would soon become proficient. When the little girl started to tire, Hari fetched an inflatable ball and taking her to the shallow end of the pool they played catch for a while.

Soon it was time for her visitors to leave. Hari quickly donned a bathrobe and slippers as she said goodbye to them as she wanted a more vigorous swim before preparing dinner. With many promises for a return visit soon, they made plans to meet for lunch in a few days' time. Seeing them safely off the premises, Hari returned to the pool for her well-earned swim. Switching on the lovely background music which she always found so restful, she swam several lengths before finishing with a few lengths of floating on her back—her favourite part!

Then she decided to have a quick sauna before dressing.

She was lying on the wooden bench in the sauna, eyes closed and humming along to the piped music when she felt a movement near her. Startled she opened her eyes and sat up to see Luc entering the sauna.

"Hello, Hari. I didn't see you there! Do you mind if I join you? My shoulders feel so tense that I thought a sauna might help before I swim a few laps."

Hari sincerely hoped that Luc could not see her blushing. She was probably red faced from the heat, anyway! Why did she react so strongly whenever he was near? He certainly was an attractive man but that didn't usually affect her—there were lots of attractive men in the army, especially in uniform, but she had never been affected like this. Keeping her eyes averted from his gorgeous form she kept her voice light inviting him in.

"Oh no I don't mind—come in. Anyway, I am cooked like a lobster, I should really be leaving."

"Don't do that! Or I shall feel guilty for disturbing you! Stay a little bit longer. Did you have fun with Amelia? She certainly is a lovely little girl."

"Yes, thanks. She is a real poppet, isn't she? I can't thank you enough for allowing her to visit. She had a great time."

"Hari, I thought I made it clear that you are welcome to invite your friends over anytime."

Unsure why she said it, Hari innocently asked, "Would that include male friends? Like a date, for instance?"

Luc looked across at her feeling shocked at the question but managed to cover up his dismay with what he hoped was a reassuring reply:

"Why, of course! You are free to do as you please, but I thought you were off males!"

"Well, I am now. But it won't last forever. Once my divorce comes through, I wouldn't mind going on the odd date I suppose. After all, I mustn't condemn all men just because I married a Lothario!"

"No, I can see that! It is just that you were so adamant that males and relationships were no go areas," he reminded her.

"Well, of course, they are at the moment. But I would not like to be alone for the rest of my life. I would miss the companionship, amongst other things." Feeling that she had already said too much, Hari got up to leave. As she prepared to pass him, Luc shifted and groaned as a spasm of pain shot through his shoulder.

"Are you alright, Luc?" She asked concernedly.

"Yes! At least it is this wretched shoulder. I think I may have trapped a nerve. Don't mind me! I am sure it will ease off eventually."

"Come here, let me see if I can massage it for you? I used to do this for Rhodri when he came back from manoeuvres. He said it helped."

Hari stood behind Luc and started manipulating the muscles in his neck, momentarily forgetting her resolution to keep a strict distance between them as her concern for his pain swept that consideration from her mind. It was only when Luc moaned in appreciation as her hands worked their magic that she realised how dangerous the situation could be. She remembered the effect these massages had on Rhodri and their subsequent lovemaking. She quickly broke off contact with Luc's muscles as if she had been burnt, her mind filled with erotic images.

"There now, I hope that helped. I really must be going," she gulped and rushed out of the sauna, leaving Luc literally stunned. Like Hari, he had found the massage very stimulating and was himself filled with erotic images of their bodies entwined. It was a huge disappointment to find himself so abruptly abandoned but a part of him could understand why she left when she did. She obviously felt a similar sexual tension between them and the consequences of them giving in to their urges would have serious implications for their future working relationship.

Luc realised that although his shoulder felt less tense, he was now in a thoroughly confused state of emotions. He knew that he was attracted to Hari. He had reacted badly to her mention of possible dates. He positively hated the image of her giving a massage to her husband—if she could produce such a magical effect on him then he had no doubt of the consequences. He was torn with jealousy. What on earth was he going to do? He had made it clear that this was to be a working relationship but that was the last thing he realised he now wanted, damn it!

Knowing that he would have to get control of himself quickly, Luc decided to have an energetic swim followed by a cold shower. He would have to get a grip on his emotions as he did not want to lose Hari. She was an excellent assistant and he really enjoyed her company. She had brought fun and laughter to his daily routine without him actually realising it. He just knew that he looked forward to each day in her company.

Chapter Nine

Although she kept in touch with her parents on a regular basis, Hari still had not forgiven them for taking Rhodri's part regarding her demand for a divorce for and believing that she was overreacting about his behaviour. When they questioned her about her plans for Christmas, she was deliberately vague but insisted that she would not be alone. She did not want them to know about Luc and his family as they would only jump to the wrong conclusions.

She was pleased to hear that her parcels had safely arrived. But she became extremely suspicious when her mother did not mention what she had organised about their own presents for Hari. Had they posted them? Since her mother had not asked for her new address this was hardly likely.

"So, Cariad, are you staying in Gstaad for the holidays?" her mother asked innocently.

"No, Mam, I am going away. I have been invited to spend Christmas with some friends," Hari replied enigmatically, trying not to give much away. "In fact, I am leaving tomorrow and my boss has given me the whole fortnight off," she added.

"Oh, that's lovely. Going somewhere nice, then? I wish you would reconsider and come home, Cariad. It won't be the same without you!"

"I know, Mam. I am sorry but there is no way I want to be near that cheating husband of mine. If I never see him again, it would be too soon!" she added vehemently.

"Aw, now, come on, love, you know you don't mean that! Of course, Rhodri has always been a bit of a flirt—he's a good-looking man after all. He can't help it if women find him attractive and chase after him now can he?" Her mother argued. "Look, mam, you don't know the half of it! Most of the time, it's Rhodri doing the chasing."

"Some men are like that, love. It doesn't mean anything. You are the one he loves, the one he married."

"It is not enough, mam. I can put up with the flirting but not with the sleeping around!"

Hari heard her mother's sharp intake of breath. This was obviously news to her.

"Are you sure, Cariad?"

"Mam, I have had my suspicions for a long time but I actually caught him at it! In our own bed, too! I have had it with his lying, cheating ways. You can't believe a word that man says, believe me. Sorry, mam, I know you think the world of him but he is not to be trusted. If that is love, I want nothing to do with it. I am better off single!"

"Oh, dear! Why didn't you say something, Cariad? If only you had told me sooner! Look, I have to go. You take care of yourself, girl, and remember that we all love you, no matter what!"

With that, Mrs Price hung up leaving Hari bemused. Something was not quite right and Hari's radar was sounding the alarm. She was glad to be leaving for Geneva the next day.

When Luc walked into the kitchen to make himself a snack and a drink, Hari was obviously distracted as she completely ignored his greeting.

"Hey, what's up? Are you okay?" He asked her.

"Oh, sorry, Luc. Did you say something?" Hari turned to look at him.

"Yes, I was wondering if you are alright. You were miles away!"

"Oh, I just had a very long phone call with my mam. Something is definitely not right. She is hiding something; I can always tell!"

"What do you mean?" Luc asked.

"Well, she thanked me for all the presents which have arrived safely but never once talked about their presents for me! I should have realised something was odd when she never asked about you or this address. It is just not like her!" she added.

"So what do you think is happening?" Luc asked.

"I have an awful feeling about this. She started singing Rhodri's praises again, so I had to put her straight. I think she finally believed me but then she went all quiet on me as if she was hiding something."

"Well, try not to worry too much. Let me make us some lunch and then why not take the afternoon off. Have you delivered Amelia's presents yet?"

"No, I thought I would do that this afternoon if you don't mind?" Just then, the intercom sounded on the gated entrance.

As Luc went to answer it, he called Hari over to look at the dark-haired man standing outside the gate.

"Hari, do you recognise this guy?"

"Damnation! That's only Rhodri bloody Morgan himself! I knew that mam was up to something. I should have known! But how did he get this address?"

"What do you want me to do?"

"I don't suppose we can pretend we are not here, can we?" Hari asked.

"Do you think he would get the message and go away?"

"No, not him, he would probably hang around outside waiting for someone to appear. I really don't want to see him, Luc!"

"Ok, why don't you go upstairs and I will speak to him?"

So, Luc talked into the intercom and pressed the release button inviting Rhodri in. As the car pulled up in front of the entrance, Luc watched a very confident man with an upright military bearing climb out of his car. He was tall and muscular, with the build of a rugby player; he had curly black hair and deep brown eyes. He was very tanned, presumably spending a lot of time outdoors. Luc noticed that the back seat of the car was piled high with presents—so Hari was right in her surmise. But how had they got his address? Well, he would soon find out.

Waiting for his visitor at the front door, Luc drew himself up to his full 6 foot 2 inches refusing to be intimidated by this burly man.

"How may I help you?" He asked politely, blocking the entrance with his frame.

"Hello, there," replied Rhodri putting on the full charm, "I am looking for my wife, Angharad Morgan. I was told that she lives here? Is she in?"

"May I ask who told you that?" Luc enquired.

"Her former employer, Elizabeth Acaster-Wilkes. Lucky thing that her slimy husband was not in when I called round or I would have planted him a right facer!" he added bullishly. "So, are you the new boss? Is she in?"

"Yes, I am her employer. I am afraid that she does not want to see you, though. You should have called."

"Oh, she will see me alright. Just tell her I won't be going anywhere until she comes down. I am a determined bastard as she well knows. I don't give up easily. I will just wait in the car while you pass on my message, shall I?"

Smug bastard, thought Luc. He knew Hari would give in. So sure of himself!

When Luc shut the door behind him, he was not surprised to see Hari sitting on the stairs, with an anxious expression on her face.

"Did you hear all that?" He asked her.

"Yes! I am going to have to see him, aren't I? Or else, he won't go away."

"I think you are right. He seems to be a determined chap. What do you want to do? He has a car load of presents to deliver. I suppose you could accept those and then send him on his way."

"I suppose I will have to! But he is not coming inside! Will you stay beside me, please? I find him quite intimidating—he refuses to take no for an answer!"

"Ok. Come on, don't be scared. He won't hurt you!"

Seeing Hari standing at the front door, Rhodri got out of the car and came to greet her with a big smile on his face.

"There you are, Cariad! Duw, but you look fantastic!" he said bending to embrace her.

But Hari put out both hands and held him off, turning her face away from his kiss.

"Aw, Cariad, don't be like that. I have missed you so much! I have come all this way to tell you how much I love you, and to take you back home with me," he added, trying once again to kiss her.

"Don't bother! I will never believe another word you say!" Hari said angrily. "I can't believe your nerve coming here like this! You are not welcome! Our marriage is over and I want a divorce. I am never coming back to you, you lying cheat!"

"Aw, you don't mean that, Cariad! Not after all we have been through. You would not throw all that away just for one silly mistake on my part, would you?" Rhodri asked beguilingly. "Aren't you going to invite me in so that we can talk in private? This is rather public for airing our differences, isn't it?"

"No, you are not welcome. There is nothing to discuss, because it wasn't just one mistake, was it? That was the only time you were caught. I am sure she wasn't the only one! Anyway, that is beside the point. I no longer love you. I no longer want to be married to you. It is time you understood that. Whether you grant me a divorce or not I am never coming back to you!"

Hari was shaking with rage and close to tears. Up to this point, Luc had stayed quietly in the background but now he stepped forward and put his arm around her shoulders, enquiring if she was okay.

"Oh, now I see it!" exclaimed Rhodri. "So, how long has this been going on? You certainly didn't waste any time moving on, did you? What about your marriage vows?" He blustered.

"There is nothing going on, as you put it!" replied Hari. "Luc is my employer and I like to think my friend. Unlike yourself, he is an honourable man and would never take advantage of a vulnerable woman. So, you can keep your mucky thoughts to yourself!" Hari bristled with anger.

"I am really sorry, but I don't think this is serving any purpose," interjected Luc. "I would ask you to kindly leave my property. It is obvious that Hari does not want to see you. She has made her position quite clear."

"This really is no concern of yours, boyo!" replied Rhodri angrily. "You have quite turned her head with your flashy house, haven't you? Well, she is still my wife and I have a right to talk to her. Her place is with me!" he added, stepping towards Luc with his fists curled, primed for a fight.

"No, Rhodri, you lost that right when you broke your marriage vows," Hari butted in. "I am no longer your concern. I would rather be single than live with you again. As for moving on—do you honestly think I want another man after the way you treated me? This job gives me back my self-respect and independence. I don't need you or your money. I certainly do not want you in my life! Sorry, but I no longer love you—in fact, I don't even like you. Now, hand over my family's presents and then be on your way."

Rhodri finally realised that he was on to a lost cause. Reluctantly, he reached into the back of his car and brought out all the parcels. When he tried to hand Hari a present from himself, she refused to accept it, slamming the door in his face. His face thunderous with rage, he stomped back to his car saying, "This isn't finished, Cariad. You haven't heard the last of this! You are my wife. Your place is by my side! You need to stop this foolish behaviour—it is not becoming!" he snarled at her.

When Rhodri's car finally disappeared out of the front gate and it closed behind him, Hari slid down to the floor, shaking uncontrollably. Luc sat down beside her and cuddled her in his arms, softly whispering, "Well done, Hari. You did well. I don't think he will be back. Come on, let me make you a drink. Actually, go and get changed—I am going to take you out for a celebratory meal. We can drop off Amelia's present enroute if you like. Come on, you need cheering up! Let's put on our glad rags and celebrate!"

Luc was absolutely right. This was just what Hari needed. She reappeared downstairs twenty minutes later dressed in smart trousers and a pretty pink sweater. She was wearing heels and walked towards him proudly with her head held high. He could see that she had been crying and his heart went out to her.

Her husband was a bully and he was not surprised that she was scared of him. Although he doubted that Rhodri would actually resort to violence, he was nevertheless intimidating. Smiling reassuringly at her, Luc helped her into her warm coat and gave her hand a squeeze of encouragement.

During the drive, he kept her entertained with hilarious stories of mishaps during some of his concerts. Before long, Hari had tears of laughter running down her face. Surely, he was exaggerating?

"Certainly not!" he replied. "I reckon I must be jinxed as trouble seems to follow me around. Maybe having you as my assistant will be a good luck charm—I hope so, as I don't know if I can stand any more costume malfunctions. I shall have to rely on you to check me over before letting me go on stage. I don't think I can take any more embarrassment."

"I don't believe half of what you are saying!" protested Hari. "You are making it up, for sure!"

"Really? I have video footage to prove otherwise!" he said, raising his eyebrows in a comical fashion.

"Oh no! When can I see them? Did you really go on stage with your flies undone? And the red lipstick mark on your cheek? Surely not the odd socks? How could you not notice them?"

"Um, I was distracted! By the lady who left the lipstick on my cheek! Luckily, no one could see the imprint of her hand on my butt! At least I hope not!" Hari guffawed in a very unladylike manner which caused Luc to innocently ask, "Sorry! But did you just snort?"

By now, Hari was convulsed with laughter and was unable to respond. She was holding her sides in agony and pleading with Luc to stop making her laugh as it hurt so much! Taking pity on her, he lapsed into silence for a while but couldn't resist teasing her further as he was enjoying her amusement.

"Of course, there was the time I was locked in my dressing room with a very amorous Italian soprano who was determined to have her wicked way with me. I have never been so scared in my life. The lady was enormous and when she threw herself on me, I thought I was going to suffocate in her bosoms! Fortunately, for me, the chaise lounge collapsed under our combined weight and I was able to roll away!"

With that, Hari was once again crying with laughter. She was seriously running out of paper hankies.

"How did you manage to escape?" She stammered through her laughter.

"Well, the stage manager happened to be passing the door when he heard the bang and her screams and he rushed in to rescue her, obviously thinking I was manhandling her! The fact that my shirt was ripped open, my face was covered in deep red kisses and I was cowering in the corner made no difference to his appraisal of the situation. My reputation as a Lothario became widespread and I took to locking my door to all intruders and keeping the key to hand to prevent any similar occurrences."

"I shall have to be your bodyguard from now on, repelling all invaders," blustered Hari.

The thought of his pint-sized assistant acting as bodyguard to his 6-foot 2-inch frame was so amusing that Luc roared with laughter.

"Now, that is a sight I would like to see!" he spluttered. "I bet you are a real tiger when roused, Angharad Morgan."

The car journey set the tone for the evening and both Luc and Hari had rarely enjoyed a dinner date quite like this one. They had quickly become the best of friends, easy in each other's company despite the undercurrent of attraction between them which they were both refusing to acknowledge.

Luc marvelled at how relaxed he was feeling, enjoying the company of this entrancing Welsh woman. She could be bossy and opinionated but at the same time, she was a really good listener. He was surprised at how much he liked sharing experiences with her even down to sharing a dessert (one large cake but two spoons so that Hari did not feel so guilty about all those calories!) which was something he had never done before. It felt quite an intimate gesture and yet somehow it felt just right.

It was only when they were turning into the garage that Hari became sombre again. Thanking Luc profusely for such a lovely evening, she went on to apologise again for dragging him into her marital difficulties. She was so embarrassed that he had to witness that scene with Rhodri. She had hoped that, by getting cleanly away from him, he would get the message that she was serious about a divorce. Hari was by nature completely without guile, she could not dissimulate, she hated secrets and surprises and she found dishonesty totally unacceptable in every form. Having had her suspicions about her husband's infidelities confirmed there was no way that she could ever forgive him. Knowing her as he did, he should realise this and just accept that the situation was irredeemable.

Luc was saddened to see all the joy drain out of Hari's face as she remembered the earlier confrontation. Determined not to let that ruin their lovely evening, he grabbed her by the hand pulling her upstairs and saying, "You go and put on some coffee and I have got some video footage which I think you will enjoy!"

Sure enough his tactics worked—half an hour later, Hari was once again convulsed with laughter to see her lovely boss caught out in embarrassing situations. The highlight of the show was the image of the amorous Italian soprano who was, as Luc mentioned, a rather buxom lady. When he raised his eyebrows at her and spread his hands in a hopeless gesture, Hari literally fell off the sofa. God, he was funny! She could not remember ever having laughed so much! "Now then, Miss! You are much too wound up to sleep. How about we have a gentle swim and a sauna before turning in? We don't need to leave too early tomorrow, but if I know Maman she will be counting the minutes!"

"Right you are! See you downstairs then!"

Hari was glad to be the first down to the pool as she was feeling self-conscious in her swimsuit, despite it being a sensible one. Dimming the lights and putting on soft music, she quickly slipped into the water before Luc arrived. He had no such qualms and Hari's breath caught at the sight of his tall, muscular body stepping into the pool. My, but he was a handsome man! Just looking at him sent ripples of desire through her body. Hari swam underwater to cool her blushing cheeks. She was not sure this was such a good idea after all.

Luc was having exactly the same thoughts. He was deeply attracted to Hari but knew instinctively that she was emotionally vulnerable and he could not take advantage of that—apart from the fact that they had a working contract which precluded any intimate relationship, more's the pity! He was having doubts as to whether this would actually be achievable. He felt so connected to Hari that he found it hard to believe that he had only known her for a few weeks. He could not imagine life without her—she made everything fun and exciting and new.

Goodness, he was smitten! He had an overwhelming urge to make love to her—he could feel himself harden just thinking about it! Never mind a hot sauna what he needed was an extremely cold shower.

Hari and Luc swam in silence both disturbed by the same tantalising thoughts, both hugely aware of each other's proximity and their near nakedness. What should have been a soothing night-time swim was turning into a sensual torture.

The sexual tension between them was palpable with each trying their hardest to hide their lustful feelings.

Hari was the first to crack—she could not stand the tension any longer. She was afraid to look at Luc in case he could guess at her thoughts.

"I think I will turn in—I am really tired! Thanks for a lovely evening, Luc. See you in the morning. Sleep well!"

With that, she scurried out of the pool, grabbed her robe and literally ran upstairs. She arrived breathless at her bedroom and had a long shower to try and release the tension which raged inside her. She was in trouble! She was in serious danger of falling in love with Luc. Not only was he a great looking guy, what woman would not be attracted to him, but he was such fun, too. He really was the whole package and she was seriously tempted by him, despite her determination to avoid all men. Damn, how had this one managed to get under her radar?

Luc meanwhile knew he would not be sleeping well at all. He would need several cold showers to dampen his ardour. He would have to be very careful not to frighten her away as he wanted to keep her in his life.

Chapter Ten

Hari spent yet another sleepless night. She re-lived her anger at Rhodri's appearance and his audacity at believing she would fall back into his arms. She was angry at her mother's connivance in his plans. She was furious that he dared to imply a relationship between herself and Luc—if only! As if that would exonerate his own behaviour over the years. She was so confused about her physical and emotional attraction to Luc. She was finding it harder to conceal her feelings but she would have to if she wanted to keep this job which she loved. She would have to keep him at arm's length and refuse any further dates, as hard as that would be. Maybe she should look for alternative accommodation since living with him was sweet agony. Yet she loved it here—she was happier than she had been for a long time.

With a shock, Hari realised the truth of this statement. Despite everything, she was happy and that was due to Luc. What a dilemma! She was almost regretting her decision to spend Christmas with him and his parents. Surely, it would be better if she kept her distance? But he filled a gap in her life which she very much needed and she wasn't sure if she was brave enough to distance herself.

When morning arrived, Hari was still debating with herself whether she should excuse herself from going to Geneva with Luc. But she could not think of a valid reason. She also did not want to stay by herself in his home especially since Rhodri had made an unwelcome appearance. It was this thought that decided her—she would go to Geneva and she would maintain a business-like distance if it killed her!

When Hari arrived in the kitchen, Luc was already cooking breakfast. He looked tired, too. What a pair! Both made a supreme effort to keep up a polite conversation with none of the easy camaraderie of the previous evening. "So, Hari, are you packed? What do you want to do with your presents from home?"

"I think I shall leave them here, thanks. I would feel embarrassed opening them at your parents."

"Maybe you would like to open them now? There's no rush to leave," suggested Luc.

"Oh, I would like that. Do you mind? I shouldn't be long. I just need to make a note of who sent what, so I can send appropriate thanks. It means that when I talk to them on Christmas Day I can thank them properly."

"I thought you would prefer that. No, I don't mind at all. Take your time."

"If you would like to help by writing notes for me, it would speed things up," suggested Hari.

"Well, if you don't think I will be in the way, I should be happy to help. You go ahead and get your little notebook ready and I shall bring in some coffee." Hari smiled to herself at his reference to her little notebook. So, he had noticed how she was always making notes. It was something she had always done from childhood. It was like a security blanket for her. As long as she had her lists, she felt in control.

When Luc appeared with two mugs of coffee, Hari was already sitting cross legged on the floor surrounded by presents, a bin liner at the ready for all the paper and packaging. She had placed her trusty notebook and pen on the sofa ready for him.

"Right then," she said, picking up the first parcel. "This one is from Cerys and Bryn." She shook the package and felt its shape trying to guess what was inside.

Luc smiled at this gesture, saying: "Hey, careful—it might be breakable!"

"I know I shouldn't do that," she replied, "but I always do! I hate surprises and would much rather have an inkling of what people have bought for me. I am a real spoilsport! My family is always telling me off about it. Well, here goes!" Hari was delighted to find a cookery book which she had wanted and a CD by the Treorchy men's choir to remind her of home.

"Oh, Duw, there's lovely. Wait until you hear this music—pure magic, it is!" She told Luc to make a note of both items and carefully put the wrapping paper into the bin liner.

The next present was from Gwyneth and Dai. They had bought her a matching hat, scarf and gloves set in lovely soft pink together with a deep pink roll neck jumper. Hari absolutely loved them and said she would wear them to travel in.

Her parents had bought her a pair of warm snow boots ideal for the winter. Little had they known that she would be staying on in Switzerland after the holidays and these would be very useful.

Her aunt and uncle had sent her a lovely home knitted aran cardigan. Hari explained that Aunty Glad's knitting was legendary—you had to put your order in early as everyone wanted something from her. She declared that she would wear the gorgeous cardigan over her pink jumper.

Next came some smaller presents from her nieces and nephews. Her nieces had chosen an assortment of gifts all with the theme of a Welsh doll—a key ring, a notebook and a pen and some chocolates.

"Magic," declared Hari. "I love the key ring. We shall take the chocolates with us for the car journey. They won't last long—I have a very sweet tooth, unfortunately. It's a good job that I am getting a lot of exercise or else I would be the size of a bus," she declared, making Luc laugh in protest.

Her nephews had sent her a collection of items for the kitchen—a recipe book, a tea towel and some wooden spoons.

The final package was from the Morgans, her in-laws. Hari opened this with trepidation. Inside was a Welsh loving spoon and a silver photo frame holding a photo of herself and Rhodri in happier times.

"Oh, no," she sighed. "Why would they do that? How can I thank them for this? What can I say? Don't they realise how difficult this is for me? Rhodri has been part of my life for years; we grew up together. This is not a whim of mine to ask for a divorce. Surely, they must know that?"

Luc did not know what to say to comfort Hari. She had been so upbeat, loving all the presents. Closing the notebook he reached down to remove the bin liner, saying:

"Come on, Hari. Don't think about that now. Let's go! Is your bag packed and ready? Do you want me to fetch it for you?"

"Oh, right! Um, no that's okay. I shall just take these up to my room and change into my new clothes. Won't be long!"

Chapter Eleven

Luc thought Hari looked completely adorable when she came downstairs clutching her small suitcase. She was wearing all of her new presents; the boots, hat, scarf and gloves! The deep pink jumper went surprisingly well with her auburn hair, contrasting beautifully with the pale pink of the bobble hat. The aran cardigan was as thick as a coat and looked comfortable to wear. He wondered whether she would keep them on the whole journey—she looked toasty, all dressed up for the snow.

As soon as they set off, Hari put her new CD into the player and they started their two-hour journey to the sounds of male Welsh voices accompanied by one female voice! Luc really enjoyed listening to the lilting sounds of the Welsh language and he particularly enjoyed hearing the sweet voice of Hari singing along.

Though he did not know the words, he hummed along to the familiar tunes.

It was a lovely journey following the scenic route around Lausanne and Lake Leman. Hari was so enthusiastic about the places they passed that Luc found himself promising to bring her back on a visit sometime. He noticed that she no longer criticised him for his choice of car but seemed to be rather enjoying the comfort of his elegant Porsche! He decided not to tease her about her conversion to expensive cars as he was enjoying the harmonious journey and did not want to disturb the peace!

By the time, they arrived at his parent's house, Luc felt he could probably give a fair rendition of the Welsh version of *All through the night/Ar Hyd Y Nos* together with the national anthem as he had heard them so many times! Hari enthusiastically told him how much she was looking forward to watching the Six Nations Rugby Championship in February. She was, of course, an avid Wales supporter and would be singing the anthem with gusto! When asked if he followed rugby, Luc said not but that he was looking forward to learning all about it. When the car turned into the driveway of a fine-looking house, Hari started to feel nervous. As Luc had predicted her hat and gloves had been quickly removed as soon as she settled into the car and now she was nervously playing with them.

"Don't worry," he said with a smile in his eyes, "they won't bite!"

As they got out of the car, the front door opened and his parents came out to greet them. They had obviously been waiting eagerly for their arrival. Luc's mother rushed to kiss and hug him, exclaiming that he looked well. Then she turned to Hari and greeted her in much the same way, saying how very pleased she was to meet her. Mr Wenger hugged his son in welcome and asked Hari's permission to do the same, being a more reserved personality than his wife. Hari was delighted to be welcomed in so friendly a manner and started to relax. As Luc and his father fetched the bags from the car, his mother ushered Hari into the house, chatting animatedly in

English with a charming French accent. Hari realised how multi-lingual this family truly was, switching between the three languages at will. She had forgotten that English was indeed not Luc's first language and it was amazing to hear him switch from French to German with such ease. She would so enjoy listening and maybe even joining in—she always relished opportunities to practise her languages.

Carrying both their bags upstairs, Luc showed Hari to her room, which had an ensuite. He explained that his room was across the corridor should she need him for anything. Suggesting that she had to freshen up, he said he would call for her in twenty minutes to take her downstairs.

Hari looked around the very pretty room designated to her. It was really tastefully done with a large comfortable double bed, a small wardrobe and dressing table. There was also a cosy armchair in the corner next to a bookshelf with an assortment of books. *Very handy if I can't sleep,* thought Hari. She quickly unpacked, freshened up in the bathroom and then collected the gifts she had brought, just as Luc knocked at her door.

"Ready?" He asked. "Here, let me help you with those parcels. You seem to have rather a lot of gifts here, Hari?"

"Some of them are food parcels, and the rest are presents for your parents," she replied.

"That's very kind of you—they weren't expecting anything, you know. Your company is all they want."

Back downstairs Hari put her presents under the beautifully decorated Christmas tree and took her food offerings through to the kitchen. Here she found Luc's parents busily preparing a lovely meal. Seeing them working in harmony Hari could see why Luc felt at home in the kitchen.

Asking if she could help in any way, she was instructed to help Luc lay the table and open the wine.

The meal proved to be a mixture of their two cultures, wiener schnitzel with roast potatoes and roast vegetables followed by clafoutis. It was absolutely delicious and when Hari complimented them on the food, asking for the recipe for the clafoutis, Luc explained about her cookery background, adding how lucky he was to have found an assistant who was also an excellent cook!

"I assume you are paying her double then, my son," exclaimed his mother. Hari grinned at Luc. She really liked his parents.

After dinner, all four helped to clear away and prepare coffee to accompany some of Hari's bara brith. Then they played board games, including team scrabble using all three languages. Hari loved this, so much better than normal scrabble! It was fun playing in teams, too, though Luc had to keep reminding her to whisper her ideas. His parents smiled fondly at the younger pair, enjoying their gentle sparring.

"Now, my favourite part of the evening," said Luc. "Family singsong time!"

"Yes, it is traditional in our little family to sing carols together on Christmas Eve," exclaimed Virginie. "Dieter, of course, accompanies us on the piano. Do you sing, Hari? We do hope you will join us!"

"I love singing as most Welsh people seem to! I sang in the school choir and at chapel, but I am afraid I was not popular as I used to keep switching between alto and soprano—it was really confusing for everyone."

So, they started singing their favourite selection of carols. When Hari was asked what her favourite carol was, she immediately said, "Silent Night." It was obviously a family favourite, too. They sang it in their various languages—English, German, French and then Hari sang a verse in Welsh: 'Dawel nos' before they harmonised the final verse in English.

The Wengers were charmed by Hari's clear sweet voice and the beautiful sound of the Welsh language. Shy at first, she soon sang with confidence and obvious enjoyment. They each chose a favourite carol and Hari was delighted when Luc chose 'O Holy Night' which she adored. It was amazing to sing with this talented family—their voices harmonised beautifully and Dieter's piano playing was exquisite. What a lovely family! She felt lucky to be spending Christmas with them.

Soon, it was time to dress for the midnight service.

"Wrap up warmly," advised Luc, "we like to walk to the service. Everything looks so beautiful in the snow with every home decked out with lights and decorations—you really must see it. We take our time on the way home just to enjoy the scenery. It is my favourite time of the year! So magical!" he added with smiling eyes.

Hari was glad of her Christmas presents from home—they came in really useful for the truly magical stroll to their charming local church. Dieter and Virginie led the way, Arms linked and greetings neighbours enroute. Luc and Hari followed in their wake, arms also linked and chatting all the way. Virginie kept casting significant glances at her husband and squeezing his arm to indicate her pleasure at Luc's new assistant and at how well they got on. She had hopes! On entering the unprepossessing church Hari was stunned into silence. The interior was quite unexpected! Used to the plain methodist chapels so common in Wales, Hari could not help but be amazed by the ornate decor of this typical Swiss church. The whitewashed walls provided an excellent backdrop for the brightly coloured statues and paintings, all decorated with sumptuous gilt edgings, and the stained-glass windows. The Stations of the Cross were depicted around the walls and were so beautifully painted that she marvelled at the artist's skill. The church positively radiated brilliant colour and Hari was captivated.

Luc smiled to see the wonder on her face—she really had such an expressive face—you knew exactly what she was thinking. He appreciated this aspect of her personality as he was too often surrounded by sycophants and insincerity. He especially liked the fact that she had taken hold of his hand, feeling a little overwhelmed by circumstances, and she was still clutching it tightly. He did not object! Somehow, it felt just right to share this magical occasion with her and his family. How she fit right in—he could tell that the instant liking between her and his parents was mutual.

Apart from the singing, the service was quite unlike the more austere methodist offering. While nothing could compare with the truly wonderful harmonising of Welsh voices, Hari could still appreciate the beautiful singing that she was hearing. The Wenger family was obviously well respected and played an integral part in this church community, their beautiful voices blending in rather than dominating the service. Hari joined in enthusiastically, completely unaware that she was still clutching Luc's hand and continually smiling up at him throughout the proceedings. She was enjoying herself so much thanks to his extraordinary man!

At the end of the church service, everyone stopped to exchange season's greetings before heading off home wards. The walk back was even more magical with that warm feeling engendered by a wonderful shared experience. Hari positively radiated happiness and energy as she enthusiastically remarked on everything she saw, still hanging on to Luc as if they were old friends.

It was nearly two in the morning by the time they arrived home, all bathed in the warm Christmas spirit. Hari exclaimed that she was far too excited to sleep despite the lateness of the hour but she promised not to disturb anyone.

"Missing my pool, Hari?" Luc quipped.

"Just a little bit!" she replied with a smile. "I shall just have to read, instead."

Despite her protests at not feeling tired, Hari did in fact sleep. The bed was so comfortable, she was so happy and relaxed, that she drifted off to sleep with no problem. She even overslept, not waking until 10 am. She awoke to the sound of music—there were carols playing in the distance and a female voice was singing gently along. With a start, Hari remembered where she was and a huge smile spread across her face. She stretched to her full height and just enjoyed a sense of wellbeing.

As comfortable as her bed was, Hari was too excited about the oncoming day to linger. So, she quickly showered and then chose her favourite dress to wear. It was made of navy velvet, calf length with 3/4 sleeves and a sweetheart neckline. She wore gold mules with two inch heels to give her a little more height and gold accessories. She chose to wear her hair long, but with the sides taken back with diamante slides. Dressed with confidence, she was ready to enjoy the day.

Luc meanwhile was already in the kitchen helping his mother prepare the vegetables. They chatted amicably in French—their language of choice when it was just the two of them.

"Alors, chéri, you are perhaps enamoured by your little Welsh assistant, non?"

"Oui, Maman. More than a little, but it is of no use. She is married, although preparing to divorce her husband. So, I must give her space. Besides, she only took the job because I included a clause in the contract that it was a business relationship only—no personal relationship allowed! Helas!"

"Oui, chéri, but it is not a written contract, hein? Also are not these contracts made to be broken if it is of your choosing?"

"But, she made it clear that she is off men, Maman!"

"Perhaps, chéri, but her heart is not completely unaffected—I have seen the way she looks at you. Pas de désespoir, mon fils!"

"You like her then, Maman?"

"Oh oui, chéri. She is exactly the woman I would choose for you!"

They quickly switched to English on seeing Hari approaching. Virginie rushed to greet her with the lovely French custom of kisses on each cheek, wishing her, "Joyeux Noel, ma chère, Hari! Que tu es belle, aujourd'hui! J'adore ta robe!"

Not to be outdone, Luc greeted her in a similar fashion whispering, "You look fantastic! I love the dress, too! Did you sleep well?"

"Do you know I did? Marvellous! I never thought I would as I get so excited about Christmas! Sorry I overslept!"

"Don't be silly," replied Virginie, "there is absolutely no rush to the proceedings today. We are en famille and take things at our leisure! Now, what can I get you?"

"Oh, please, let me help. I really would like to," begged Hari.

"Well, then, why not have a croissant and a coffee and then you can help me in the kitchen. It will be nice having a female to chat, too. No, don't be offended, mon fils," she countered, seeing Luc's outraged face, "you know how we girls like to chat. With you and papa, I am usually outnumbered!"

"Okay. At least, sit down and have your breakfast first, Hari. Here, I shall serve you and then you are at Maman's disposal. I shall go and find Vati to see if he wants to play a game of chess if I am no longer needed," he stated, with a smile to show he wasn't offended in the slightest.

Having obediently eaten her breakfast, Hari quickly cleared away and then offered herself as Virginie's sous-chef!

"But first, ma chère, you must cover up that really beautiful dress! It is such a lovely colour on you! Très jolie!" said Virginie handing Hari a large apron. "Now, you can prepare the roast potatoes s'il te plaît!"

Hari replied in perfect French and Virginie was even more delighted in her son's choice of assistant—she spoke languages, she had a lovely singing voice, she was down to earth and ready to help—parfait! Oh, how she wished that they would disregard that dreadful clause. She would get to know this lovely young Welsh woman a little better and see if she was as smitten with her son as he seemed to be with her.

By the time the ladies had everything prepared and in the oven, Luc had reappeared offering them a drink. It was suggested that they went into the lounge to open some presents. Dieter was already putting on some festive music and had a bottle of champagne at the ready. Luc was delighted to see that Hari was getting on well with his mother. She looked so relaxed and at home, especially wearing that oversized apron, that it warmed his heart. His two favourite women, he thought with a shock—when had that happened?

When they joined Dieter in the lounge, he gave them all a flute of champagne toasting them with a 'Prost! Santé! Cheers!' which drew a laugh from everyone.

Hari countered with 'hwyliau' and then 'Nadolig Llawen/ Merry Christmas'. In Hari's honour, Dieter had found a male voice choir singing carols to play as background music, stating that he hoped she would sing along should she feel the urge.

"I probably won't be able to stop myself, so you have been warned!" she replied with her ready smile.

"Alors, les cadeaux!" said Virginie. "Luc, mon fils, you will do the honours? Guests first, I believe!"

So, Luc sought amongst the stack of presents which surrounded the tree and found one with Hari's name on it. This was from his parents.

"For me? Oh, you shouldn't have! Really it is enough to be invited as your guest," she protested.

"Nevertheless, it is our pleasure. We enjoy giving presents—it is the best part of the season, don't you agree?" smiled Dieter. "Go on, open it! Let us see if we guessed the right present from your reaction."

Hari excitedly unwrapped the beautifully wrapped present having first fondled it and shaken it to see if she could pick up any hints. Luc burst out laughing, explaining to his parents that this was her customary behaviour.

"Well, Hari," he laughed, "any clues?"

"It's soft! But I don't want to spoil the surprise by guessing," she said. Then she exclaimed in delight as she revealed a lovely soft blue pashmina. "Oh, how beautiful! I love it! Thank you so much." She draped it around her shoulders to model it and to show her delight in the present. Then she went and kissed Virginie and then Dieter by way of thanks.

"Well chosen, Liebling," Dieter said to his spouse.

"Now, it is my turn," said Luc. "Here, Hari, a little something from me. I think you will like it!" he said with a smile.

Luc's gift consisted of two parcels, one boxed and one gift wrapped. "Can you guess?" He asked as she did her usual performance.

"A book of some sort? But I don't know what is in the box."

"Open it and see, then!" he laughed.

The book turned out to be just that, but a large leather-bound notebook.

"For your lists!" he laughed.

The box revealed the most beautiful fountain pen she had ever seen. "Oh, Luc! I absolutely love it! Thank you so much." She hurled herself at him and gave him a huge hug and a kiss before collecting herself and blushing in embarrassment.

"Well, if that's the reception I get, remind me to keep you stocked up!" he quipped.

Hari insisted that she should give out her presents next. She was so happy, a little high on champagne, and general euphoria! Ironically, she had chosen a similar present for Virginie, a shawl in beautiful shades of blue, which delighted her. Dieter was equally pleased with his cravat which she had chosen to match the sweater Luc had bought his father.

Next she handed Luc his present. She had chosen a merino sweater in an unusual purple shade, a colour that she was sure he would never have chosen himself. But with his dark blond hair and deep blue eyes, she knew it would suit him. When he tried it on, she was pleased to note how good it looked. With all the presents opened and the wrappings gathered up and binned, Virginie went to check on lunch. Hari put her champagne to one side fearing that she was getting tipsy—she would not have any more until she had eaten something. Dieter asked her if she would sing to his accompaniment on the piano. Maybe Luc would join in, too? With such a musical family it was inevitable that music was very much part of each day.

Hari sang *Calon Lan* and *Ar Hyd y Nos.* Then Luc and his father duetted *O Tannenbaum, Still, Still, Still* and *Es ist ein Ros entsprungen* so beautifully that tears sprang to Hari's eyes. Virginie came in and kissed both her men with fondness, congratulating them on their fine performance.

"Danke sehr, now it is your turn, mein Liebchen!" exclaimed Dieter. Virginie sang a beautifully haunting carol called *Le grand Dieu d'amour* which Hari had never heard before. What a talented family! They were so much fun to be with.

Then Virginie called a halt to proceedings saying lunch was ready.

Chapter Twelve

Christmas dinner in the Wenger household proved to be delicious and heart-warming. Hari delighted in the company of these friendly people. She loved the way the conversation switched effortlessly between languages. There was so much laughter—she felt really at ease with them. To her astonishment, she realised that she had not thought of her own family until Luc suggested that she might like to ring them while they cleared the dishes. Then he would take her for a walk to help digest that enormous meal.

So, Hari phoned home in private and spoke to her parents, then her sisters. Her mother was careful not to mention Rhodri until the end of the call when she expressed her concern that Hari had obviously moved on so soon. She was repeating Rhodri's conviction that Hari was involved with Luc thus sharing the blame for their break up. Hari refused to be drawn on the subject telling her mother that firstly Rhodri had no right to criticise as he had broken their marriage vows on numerous occasions, and secondly what she did with her life from now on was her own concern. She firmly denied there being any involvement between her and Luc saying he was her boss.

"But, Hari, Cariad—you are living with him all alone in that great big house. And he is a looker! And single!"

"Mam, this is the twenty-first century not the dark ages. I am a grown woman. There is nothing going on between us—more's the pity," she mumbled under her breath. "Now, I have to go. Love to you all and thanks for the lovely presents. When we next talk, please do not mention that cheating ex-husband of mine, alright!"

When Hari joined the others in the kitchen, Luc could see the tension in her face. So, he quickly took her by the arm and said, "Right then, Mrs Morgan. How about that walk I promised you? Maman, Vati, do you want to join us?"

"Non, merci, chéri. We shall be quite happy having a sit down. You young ones go and enjoy yourselves. Why don't you take your ice skates down to the lake? If Hari wears thick socks my skates might fit her."

"How about it, Hari? Do you skate?"

"Not very well, but I would love to try!" she replied. "But I better change into something more comfortable for that. Give me ten minutes, would you?"

"No problems. Take your time. I shall have a look in the garage for the skates."

When they reached the lake half an hour later, there were several couples skating around. Luc helped Hari put on his mother's rather large skates which she padded out with thick socks and then donning his own skates he led her gingerly onto the lake. She gripped his hand so tightly that he feared it would stop his circulation. Turning to face her, he took both her hands in his, and skating backwards he gently pulled her along. Gradually, Hari found her balance and managed to skate along reasonably well. She was fine if she stopped worrying about what her legs were doing but the moment she thought about the ice, she slipped.

Gaining confidence, she pushed off too hard, her feet went in different directions, and she fell pulling Luc with her. Landing heavily on the ice and just managing not to fall on Hari herself, Luc looked over at her and said, "Déjà vu? I seem to remember being in a similar situation the first time we met. Don't you?"

"Yes sorry, Luc. I was doing so well, too. Can you help me up?"

"Of course," he said, "but first, I also remember doing this!"

And he bent his head and kissed her gently on the lips. That was a mistake. It was even more powerful than the first time, confirming that his feelings for Hari were not mistaken. She looked equally dazed. *So, not unmoved,* he thought.

Should that give him hope?

Leaning down he helped her to her feet, whispering, "Tu fais tourner mon coeur! Je suis fou de toi!" Hari's legs were shaky, she was not sure if this was due to the ice skates or that kiss. Why was she so affected by his touch, his kiss, his nearness? Could she really keep to a purely platonic relationship? Did she really hear those loving words he just uttered and did that mean he was also troubled by her?

So many thoughts rushed through her head—she really did not know how to react to him. She decided that she would just have to follow his lead as he was the boss.

Luc was also having trouble controlling his thoughts. Why had he kissed her? Why did he have this overwhelming compulsion to kiss her? What must she be thinking of him? She was still married, after all! As her employer, he really should not be taking advantage like this. But she drew him like a magnet—he had never felt like this before. Feeling slightly ashamed for taking advantage of her, Luc decided to resume a less intense approach.

"You really must stop throwing yourself at me like that, Hari! I shall start to think that you fancy me!" he joked. "You really don't have to knock me down if you want a kiss you know!"

He got just the reaction he expected. "Why, you cheeky sod! Think a lot of yourself, don't you?"

"Just a bit!" he grinned in response. "Come on, let's take these skates off—I don't want any more bruises; I wish you would choose somewhere more comfortable next time you want to throw yourself at me!!"

That got him a thump on the arm from Hari who was, for once, speechless.

They walked home in relative harmony deliberately avoiding any mention of that kiss. Luc showed Hari some of his favourite places and talked about his early childhood growing up in this neighbourhood. He asked Hari questions about her childhood, growing up in Wales. Listening to her reminiscing, he realised how much an integral part of her life Rhodri had been. Could she really cut herself adrift from him?

Changing the subject which was becoming so uncomfortable to her, Hari said how much she liked his parents and how much she was enjoying this visit. Pleased that she was enjoying herself, Luc talked about some of the treats to come. Boxing Day traditionally saw his family hosting a large party for friends and neighbours. Then they would be invited to reciprocal parties. The biggest event was the New Year's Eve Charity Ball. An enormous event attended by a lot of dignitaries and stars. The proceeds from the ticket sales and the auction of promises would all go to charity. It was one of the biggest events on the annual calendar.

When Hari expressed concern that she would feel out of her depth, Luc reassured her that he would not abandon her and that she would have a great time spotting celebrities.

Back at the house, Virginie had put together a light buffet so that people could help themselves. When Hari asked whether she could help with the preparations for their party the next day, she was assured that it was all being handled by outside caterers.

A pleasant evening was spent watching festive films before having an early night. Luc held Hari back and gave her an extra Christmas present. "I do hope you like it and that it is the right size," he said cryptically.

Inside a large box, beautifully wrapped in tissue paper, was the loveliest pale green chiffon ball gown embellished with silver spangles.

"Oh, my goodness, Luc. This is beautiful! Is this the one I was admiring when we went Christmas shopping? But I can't possibly accept such a generous present," she said hesitantly.

"Yes, you can! It is for the Charity Ball. I knew you wouldn't have anything suitable and anyway, what girl can refuse a glamorous ball gown. You will be like Cinderella! I didn't dare buy you shoes but if you need some, I will take you shopping."

"Oh, Luc! This is so gorgeous. I can't wait to try it on."

"I hope it fits!" he replied.

"Give me ten minutes and then come to my room and I will show you what it looks like!" Hari said excitedly, not realising the implications of her invitation.

When Luc tapped at her door a short while later, Hari was inside the dress clutching it against her as she had been unable to reach the back fastenings. "I need help, Luc," she said, turning her bare back towards him.

"Yes, I can see that! Here, allow me!" Bending down, he carefully pulled up the zipper trying not to look at her semi-nakedness. "Right give me a twirl."

"Just a moment! I need to find some heels first. Well, what do you think?"

"Stunning, Hari, you look incredible. How does it feel? Does it fit okay?"

"Like a glove! Oh, Luc, thank you so much. I absolutely love it! I can't wait to wear it!" Hari reached up to kiss his cheek in thanks.

"Are the shoes okay or do we need to go shopping?"

"Well, if you can bear it, I would love to buy some special shoes. I adore going around the sales. I really don't mind going alone, though as I know you men hate shopping."

"Oh, I don't mind as long as we set a time limit. I will even treat you to lunch. Besides, I need a few items myself. Right, do you want me to unzip you or can you manage?"

"Yes please. I had better hang it up carefully. Oh, I can't wait to wear it," she said excitedly.

Having helped her with the zipper, Luc hurriedly bade her goodnight as he did not trust himself being so close to her tantalising body. He was going to need a very cold shower after that vision!

Chapter Thirteen

Breakfast the next day was a very leisurely affair. Virginie had told Hari to get up as late as she wished. Breakfast would be very informal—every man for himself so to speak. Guests would be arriving from 14.00 and the party would last until the early hours. People generally came and went as they pleased, with no strict timings involved. It was a lovely relaxed affair of many years standing and Hari was very welcome to participate for as long as she liked. If she preferred to excuse herself, that would also be acceptable. She should feel at home to come and go as she pleased.

Hari was really grateful that her presence would not be relied upon. She wasn't sure how she would cope in a room full of people where she didn't know anyone and with the language differences. So she was glad to have an escape plan should she need it.

However, she need not have worried. Like the Wengers themselves, their friends and neighbours were friendly and relaxed people. They made Hari welcome speaking English until they found that she was quite able to converse in French or German. As she struggled with the less familiar Swiss German, this was avoided, although some guests took delight in teaching her a few words and phrases. Hari reciprocated by teaching them some Welsh. She had particular fun getting them to pronounce her full name. Luc circulated, catching up with old friends. He always enjoyed this Boxing Day gathering as his busy schedule precluded his keeping in touch with people on a regular basis. He was relieved to see that Hari was also enjoying herself, captivating people with her lively personality and ready laugh. He had inadvertently found a gem of an assistant, he realised. What a lucky day it turned out to be when he rescued his novice skier! That reminded him that he was keen to fit in some skiing with Hari to see how much she had progressed since taking lessons. He would make sure to schedule some fun time as soon as they got back to Gstaad. What better way to see in the New Year.

As Virginie predicted, people kept arriving until well into the early hours. The caterers did a wonderful job of keeping glasses topped up and continuously circulating with trays of delicious food. It was well after two in the morning before the last guest left and they were able to fall exhausted but happy into their beds, with many invitations accepted for the forthcoming days.

Looking back, Hari could not believe how quickly the time went. She had never enjoyed herself so much. Every day saw an invitation to some event or gathering. She was pleased at how easily she recognised people and remembered their names. She was also relieved to find that many of them would also be attending the Charity Ball, so she would not be entirely friendless after all. As much as she loved spending time with Luc, she realised that he had obligations to circulate at these events and he would not want to have to escort her everywhere. At least, she now felt more confident that she would not be a wallflower sitting alone in the corner when he did his duty circulating as several of her new acquaintances had already claimed at least one dance with her.

True to his word Luc had taken Hari shoe shopping. He gave her a strict time limit and she set herself a budget as there were so many sales that she was in danger of being overwhelmed. She found the perfect shoes for her Cinderella dress plus a matching bag. She also treated herself to some silver drop ear-rings. Luc had left her to her own devices while he ran some errands of his own, arranging to meet up for lunch.

New Year's Eve arrived and Hari could not contain her excitement. She did indeed feel like Cinderella, especially since Virginie took her off to a beauty salon which she had booked in advance for the complete works! Hari had never felt so indulged in her life. Virginie insisted on paying for everything declaring that she had always wanted a daughter to share things with, and while Luc was a wonderful son, there were times when only a female companion would do. She told Hari how very much they enjoyed her company and hoped she would be a regular visitor. Luc was often too busy to keep in regular touch so Virginie was hoping that Hari could fill that breach and asked if she minded exchanging mobile numbers and email addresses.

After a few hours of pampering, Hari had never felt so good. Virginie then surprised her even further by taking her to a very elegant restaurant for lunch, "So, that we can be seen and admired, ma chère!" she smiled happily. Judging from the reaction of many of the other diners who stopped by their table to compliment them and pass on New Year wishes, it was money well spent. Virginie basked in the adulation and flirted harmlessly with many of her male acquaintances. Hari was shocked to realise just how famous Virginie was in certain circles. She felt quite a country bumpkin in comparison. One thing was for sure—if she managed to hold on to this job, it would do wonders for her self-esteem and worldliness.

By the time the ladies arrived back home, they were firm friends. Virginie insisted on overseeing Hari's outfit for the evening offering her a loan of any accessories she might need. She was enchanted by the dress and hid a secret smile when Hari innocently revealed that it was a present from Luc. Her son was truly smitten, much to her delight. She loved this natural young woman, so different from his previous assistants with their cool elegance and stiff manner. The men were looking handsome in their black dinner jackets with black bow ties. They were having a brandy to fortify themselves as the ladies entered the room. What a vision of loveliness! They declared themselves lucky men to be escorting such beautiful creatures and kissed them gently on the cheeks so as not to spoil their immaculate make-up. Both declined the offer of a drink, so the men didn't linger over theirs.

On seeing the beautiful venue held at the Grand Hotel Kempinski, Hari did indeed feel like Cinderella arriving at the Ball with her handsome prince. She gazed around in wonder not quite believing that she, little Angharad Price from South Wales, was actually attending such a glamorous event. As an army officer's wife, she had attended many balls and functions but none as magnificent as this one. Listening to the many languages being spoken around her, she appreciated just how big an international event this was.

Not being a stranger to these grand events, Luc took it all in his stride, greeting his numerous acquaintances and introducing a completely overawed Hari who hung on to his arm as if her life depended on it. She gradually started to relax as she recognised some of their friends and the pressure on Luc's arm lessened.

Then she was whisked away by a neighbour into a promised dance.

From then on, Luc hardly saw her as she was claimed for dance after dance. He was likewise doing his duty dancing with the wives and daughters of many of his friends. His heart stopped when a loud voice called his name:

"Luc, mi amore! How lovely to see you 'ere! We dance, no?"

It was Maria Benedetto, a vibrant soprano whom he had dated a few years' ago. Their split was acrimonious to say the least. She had a determined look about her that Luc remembered well. He was well and truly trapped!

"Maria! How lovely to see you, too, ma chère. I did not know you were in Geneva."

"I arrive last night. I am to sing at the New Years' Day concert. But why not you?"

"My assistant left in rather a hurry this month and there has been a mix up with bookings. She left my diary in rather a mess—so I sadly never got the invitation for this year's event."

"Non importa! You can duet with me, caro!"

"Oh, how kind of you to suggest that, Maria, but I am leaving tomorrow. I have engagements already booked," he said with relief.

"Now we dance!" she commanded, annoyed to be thwarted in her first attempt to get closer to him.

As they danced, Maria did everything she could to get her hooks into Luc. She flirted outrageously with him, laughing so loudly that she drew attention from all sides—all part of her masterplan. When the dance finished, she clung to his arm greeting people together as if they were very much a couple again. Luc felt trapped—he knew Maria's behaviour from past experience and could see what she was doing. Just then, he caught Hari's eye and mouthed, "Help!"

Excusing herself from her group, she headed straight for Luc saying, "Luc, there you are! I have been looking all over for you. What about that dance you promised me?" She asked innocently.

"Luca, who is this child?" Maria hissed dangerously.

"Oh, Maria—may I introduce you to Angharad Morgan, my new assistant. Hari, this is Maria Benedetto, an old friend. Now, if you will excuse us, I have indeed promised her a dance."

Releasing his arm from her grasp he practically dragged Hari on to the dancefloor with huge relief.

"Merci, mon ange! I was worried for a while, there!"

She asked with a giggle, "Who is that maneater?"

"Believe it or not, that is an old girlfriend of mine. I made the mistake of dating her a few years' ago and she was impossible to shake off when things turned sour. I get the distinct impression that she wants me back!"

"Do you need me to hide you?" Hari laughed at his horrified expression.

"Not even your Welsh magic could work that, unfortunately, she is a very determined woman and not easily put off as I know to my cost."

"Look, she is watching us closely. Why don't we pretend that we are an item—after all, if she thinks you are in a relationship she will have to give up, won't she?" Hari suggested.

"She might, but I doubt it! Worth a go, though!" Luc replied. He was completely taken aback when Hari danced him into the corner of the room and backing him against a wall she stood on tiptoe and pulled his head down for a very long kiss. His arms wrapped around her of their own accord. They were lost in the moment. When they finally pulled apart, they were both quite breathless. Luc kept his arms around Hari while he whispered in her ear, "She is still watching us. I don't know if we convinced her—what do you suggest we do next?"

Hari shivered as she felt his lips caress her neck.

"I think you are doing very well without any help from me! If you carry on like that, I shall be dragging you into secluded room and having my wicked way with you!" She said huskily.

"Oh, oh, don't look now but the enemy is approaching. Quick kiss me!" Luc replied urgently.

As he pulled Hari into an embrace which had her limbs melting into submission, they heard an angry Italian voice from behind them: "Luc! What is the meaning of this? Why are you kissing this child woman?"

Breaking reluctantly apart, Luc kept Hari clutched against his chest and faced a very angry Maria.

"Mmm? Oh sorry, Maria. I was a bit distracted there!" he said huskily.

"What do you mean by this outrageous behaviour in public?" She queried.

"Oh! Why? Because I am totally bewitched by this captivating creature. She has me completely under her spell and I hope I never escape!" he replied dreamily, planting little kisses on the captive Hari. "I am sorry—did you want something?" He asked distractedly, looking deeply into Hari's eyes, willing her not to laugh at his obvious playacting.

"But, Luc, this is not acceptable. I come expressly to invite you to duet with me and you ignore me for this child woman."

"Sorry, Maria. But why do you keep calling her that foolish name? I can assure you she is definitely no child but all woman," he replied, running his hands up and down Hari's curves. "Most assuredly very much a woman!" he purred. Seeing that he was refusing to leave his dreadful little assistant, the Italian woman stamped her foot angrily and stormed off mouthing obscenities under her breath.

"Has she gone?" Hari asked, interrupting Luc's caresses. "You can stop now, Luc!" she added as he continued to buss his lips down her neck.

"Oh, must I? Spoilsport! I was having such a nice time!" he replied dreamily.

"Thank you, Hari, I owe you a favour after that showdown."

He finally released Hari with great reluctance. They both needed a moment to retain their equilibrium and get their breathing under control. They could no longer deny that there was nothing between them—the attraction was evident and the sparks that they set off within each other were growing. Luc was regretting the strict business relationship clause and was not sure how he should approach this matter with Hari. Just give it time! He told himself.

Grabbing Hari by the hand, he suggested that they had another dance before the auction of promises. He had seen so little of her during the evening as she had been in demand with no end of dancing partners.

Hari felt she was floating in Luc's arms. She had nearly lost control of herself when kissing him and was not joking when she quipped about having her wicked way with him. It was becoming an overwhelming obsession—every time they kissed, it got harder to resist him. She was not sure whether she really would be able to keep to a purely business relationship—she certainly did not want to!

The dancing was momentarily suspended while the stage was set up for the auction of promises. Guests sought out their seats at the various tables where drinks and light snacks were available. Luc and Hari joined his parents at their table.

Hari asked him excitedly, "Are you bidding for anything, Luc?" Hari asked him excitedly.

"That would be telling!" he winked at her. "You will have to wait and see!"

The first auction was a day's skiing for four people with a guide, plus a three-course meal and drinks. The bidding was quick and was snapped up at huge expense by a British businessman.

Then came a succession of outstanding auctions, a meal for four at one of the most expensive restaurants in Paris, a cookery course for four at a Michel Roux academy, a day's shopping with your own stylist, a weekend for two at a spa resort, a singing lesson with the famous French Soprano Virginie Duplessis (Hari's ears pricked up at this!), a date with the handsome Sebastien! (What?! That's Luc!).

The list was endless.

Luc bid for the spa weekend and won to Hari's delight. But what a huge amount of money he had spent! When his own auction came up, she was amazed at the number of women bidding outrageously large sums to go on a date with him. Just as the gavel was about to come down a loud Italian voice doubled the bid—oh no, Maria had just bought herself a date with Luc! That woman, would she never give up. The look that she threw across at Luc did not bode well for him. Hari felt that this last surprise had spoilt a lovely evening. She did not trust the Italian woman, there was something malevolent about her. She worried how Luc would handle it and wished she had enough money to outbid her. Seeing her anxious face, Luc gave her fingers a reassuring squeeze. They would think of something!

The auction was deemed the best ever. The money raised far exceeded last year's total largely due to the most generous bid by Signora Benedetto. Secretly, Luc wondered how Maria could afford such an amount—life must certainly have improved since they parted. Was it wrong of him to hope that she would default on the bid? Well, he wasn't going to worry about that now as the dancing had started up again and there was a certain young Welsh lady who claimed his attention.

The Ball was a huge success. When Luc drove his family home, with a rather tipsy Hari leaning against his shoulder singing softly to herself, his parents smiled at her obvious enjoyment of the evening. They talked quietly to each other replaying some of their favourite moments. When Virginie worriedly asked Luc about Maria's reappearance, he tried to shrug off his own concern. Hari perked up at this moment saying, "It's alright, Virginie. I convinced her that Luc and I am an item. I shall make it plain that he is not free, so back me up on this if you get the chance," she giggled.

"Oh, chérie, however did you manage that?" She queried innocently.

"Oh, let's just say we put on a good floor show! She got the message alright. Only problem—she was so annoyed, she went and bid the highest at the auction."

"Yes, well I am hoping that she was a bit reckless and will have to rethink," said Luc. "I can't believe she can afford that sort of money. So, I am keeping my fingers crossed for a withdrawn bid!"

Hari nuzzled against him whispering with a wicked grin, "I would have bid for you but it all went too fast for me! Also I don't have that sort of money. Sorry!"

"You can have a date with me anytime for free!" he whispered into her hair, which gave her a delicious warm feeling inside.

Since Hari had kicked off her high heels, Luc gallantly carried her into the house. Putting her down in the hallway, he gently tapped her on her bottom and said, "Bed for you, Cinderella! Don't rush to get up—we are in no hurry to leave." Wishing everyone goodnight, saying how very much she had enjoyed herself; Hari was so happy that she kissed them all twice and then danced her way to bed, singing, 'I could have danced all night', as she went.

Luc wished his parents a goodnight and decided to make himself a coffee before retiring himself. He needed some quiet time to himself to recover some of his equilibrium. He knew without a doubt that he was in love with Hari and he was not sure what to do about it.

Chapter Fourteen

It was well after lunch before Luc and Hari took their leave. They took a fond farewell of Luc's parents with many promises and assurances that they would visit again soon. The car was packed with so many parcels that Hari quipped, "Anyone would think it is Christmas!"

She was feeling a little subdued to be leaving. She had had such a lovely time, and the Ball was everything a girl could dream of. It had taken her a long time to get to sleep as she kept reliving the evening, especially her clinch with Luc. Just thinking about him brought her out in goosebumps and it took every ounce of willpower not to go to his room and have her wicked way with him.

She was also feeling low as her mother had called to wish her a Happy New Year—slightly annoyed that Hari had made no effort to contact her family over the holidays. They were feeling neglected especially as she usually spent the holidays with them. Now, she was far away in a foreign land with strangers with not a thought for her family and estranged from her husband. It just wasn't right! Hari's mother made her opinion abundantly clear. So, now Hari was feeling guilty because she had not given them a thought since Christmas Day. But didn't she have a right to her own life? How could she go home to such a close community when she and Rhodri were at odds? She was only just realising how difficult things would be in the future if they divorced. Not if, when! She corrected herself.

She could not take him back, the lying, cheating git!

These thoughts were racing through her mind as Luc drove out of Geneva.

He asked, "You are quiet, Hari, Everything alright?"

"Yes. No! My mam had a right go at me! Understandably as I haven't given them a thought. But I resent her being right. I have had such a lovely time and she has spoilt it! I have been so unhappy for so long—I just didn't tell anyone about Rhodri's bad behaviour. Apart from his sleeping around, he wasn't nice to me—always belittling me, making me feel small and useless, and lording it over me. I was really beginning to dislike him before I caught him in bed with a friend. But I never said a word to anyone because they all think the world of him. So, now I am being blamed for throwing away years and years of friendship. But that's just it—we should never have married. We were good friends. More like brother and sister, I see that now. Trouble with Rhodri is that he likes to control things—the minute I went abroad without him, he couldn't stand it. I actually enjoyed my time away—I was just never brave enough to make the break."

Luc reached over to grip her hand reassuringly.

"I just never realised how hard this is going to be for me when I go home. He has always been part of my home. How am I going to cope? But I can't live with him! I don't want to be married to him anymore! I want someone to love me, the real me, to cherish me, to treat me well not to belittle me and make me feel bad."

With that, Hari started to sob quietly. Luc reached into the dash and passed her a hanky letting her sob out her hurt, wishing he could comfort her, but knowing that she had to exorcise her own demons.

When she finally got control of herself, Hari apologised for spoiling what had been a truly lovely week. She appreciated how welcome Luc's parents had made her feel. She loved meeting their friends and neighbours. Everyone was kindness itself. She would always remember it with fondness, especially the Ball.

Luc brushed aside her thanks, saying how much her parents had enjoyed her company. He told her not to worry about Rhodri for the moment. To give herself time to heal, time to work out what she wanted for herself, what was right for her and not for her family. He made such sense that Hari felt calmer.

"Anyway," added Luc, "I mean to keep you so busy that you won't have time to brood. We have an extremely busy schedule ahead of us you will certainly be earning your salary!"

They arrived back in Gstaad late afternoon.

"Ah, it's good to be home!" sighed Hari.

"I'm glad that is how you feel about it! I am rather fond of it myself! Right, why don't you rustle up something to eat while I bring in all the bags? Then, if you can bear it, I need to check my emails and update my calendar. There are some important dates in next week's schedule that I need to remind myself of. After that, I shall need a swim and a sauna to unwind."

"Ok, that sounds good to me. I shall see what I can rustle up."

Hari was pleased to be able to get back into a work routine. She really enjoyed her Christmas break despite her mother's comments but now she was just relieved to be back at work. She hoped to keep so busy that she would not have time to brood over her personal life...She was determined to make the most of this fantastic opportunity.

So when Luc came down after taking up the bags, she had a light meal set out for them both in the kitchen. They chatted amiably while they ate, keeping to safe topics and then they went into the office to sort out the post. Hari enjoyed bringing her wall chart up to date. Luc's first engagement was at the weekend to sing in the New Year's concert in Rome. Accommodation had been booked and he would be driving himself. She did not know if she was expected to accompany him.

Then Jason Greene was visiting during that coming week to do some recordings with Luc. The following week, Luc was due in Rome for a New Year's Gala performance. Hari noticed that travel and accommodation had been booked, but she would have to confirm details.

March saw him travelling to Paris for a week of concert dates. Again, she would need to confirm booking details. She happily made notes in her new notebook and updated the wall chart. She was in her element organising his calendar and was so engrossed that she didn't hear Luc talking to her.

"Hari, do you want a coffee break? How are you getting on?"

"Oh, thanks, Luc. Fine! Just updating your calendar. I need to check on your bookings for Rome and Paris—it looks as if travel and accommodation have been sorted, but I need to confirm everything to my liking. It says that two rooms have been booked for Rome and a suite of rooms for Paris—does that sound right to you? I don't know what your usual arrangements are?"

"Oh, didn't I say? You will be coming with me, of course. That is why there are two rooms. Is that okay?"

"Really! I didn't realise that I would be travelling with you. Oh, I have always wanted to go to Rome and Paris. Thank you so much, Luc. I love this job!" Hari said excitedly.

"You are welcome!" he smiled at her enthusiasm. "I found it easier to have my assistant with me when I travel. It helps to have a ready date with me if I need to avoid some of the more amorous leading ladies."

"Do I get to be your bodyguard again? Or do we need to pretend to be an item like with the Italian lady?"

"We shall have to play it by ear, as they say!" Luc enigmatically replied. "Now, I am going to have a swim and a sauna and an early night if you care to join me?"

"Let me finish up here and I may come down later," Hari replied, not sure she could cope with seeing his honed, muscular body in such minimal clothing without wanting to jump on him. Her self-restraint was certainly wearing thin.

Luc was doing leisurely strokes up and down the pool. He had switched on the subdued blue lighting and soft music was gently playing. He could feel the tension slowly releasing from his body. Although he had enjoyed his stay in Geneva, he relished the peace and serenity that his own home gave him. The calm atmosphere which he had deliberately manufactured helped him to unwind. Was it wrong to love a home so much?

He was so lost in his own thoughts that he was unaware of Hari's presence until she slipped into the water. He felt his pulse accelerate at the sight of her, his earlier calmness disappearing. *Maybe it wasn't such a good idea to invite her to join him,* he thought. There was only so much temptation a man could take after all!

Determined to maintain a safe distance between them, Luc decided to use the sauna, hoping to calm his pulse rate and erotic thoughts about his lovely assistant. He prayed that she would not follow him because his self-restraint was weakening daily.

Hari was also questioning her own judgement. Why did she give into the temptation of being in such close proximity to his enticing body? She was no saint! How long could she resist the magnetic pull towards him? Despite finding this evening swim relaxing, she felt her pulse racing at the mere thought of him. With a groan of despair, Hari decided to quit the battlefield before she lost control. Luc was having similar thoughts of making an equally cowardly withdrawal. He was starting to doubt whether taking Hari to Rome and Paris would work on a personal level. As he exited the sauna, Hari was just leaving the pool. Gosh, she was gorgeous! How he wished things could be different between them. He waited until she had left the room and then decided to cool off in the pool for a while.

Upstairs in her room, Hari admitted to herself that she had fallen for her handsome employer hook, line and sinker! She did not think she could stand the sexual tension between them any longer and decided that she should take the initiative, as Luc was so clearly a gentleman.

Having showered and washed her hair, Hari carefully brushed it until it fell in long auburn waves down her back. She donned a pastel pink silk nightgown and lightly sprayed herself with perfume. Breathing deeply, she listened for sounds that Luc had retired for the night. Tiptoeing along the corridor, she waited outside his room and listened at his door. All was quiet—now was her moment! Taking a deep breath, it took all her courage to open the door. Luc was sitting up in bed reading. He looked up in surprise to see Hari silhouetted in the doorway, like all his dreams come true.

"Hari! Is there a problem?" He asked nervously hoping she couldn't see how pleased he was to see her.

"There could be, Luc!" she answered huskily. "If I said I had an itch, what would you do?" She asked enigmatically.

"Well, I guess I would offer to scratch it!"

"Oh thank you, that is what I was hoping you would say," she replied coming towards the bed.

To Luc's utter amazement, Hari slipped into the bed beside him and quietly whispered exactly where she itched! Luc was astounded to realise just what she was implying. He was even more surprised when her actions followed her words and she leant over to kiss him, her silk covered breasts brushing against his chest. Suddenly, all restraint between them was gone and their coming together was fast and passionate.

"Oh, thank goodness, we have got that out of the way," purred Hari. "Now, we can get back to being comfortable with each other again. I felt like Mt Etna every time you looked at me, so close to eruption it was painful."

"I know just what you mean!" exhaled Luc, cuddling her to him. It felt so good to finally have her in his arms. He was

133

so grateful that she had taken the initiative as his resolve to behave like a gentleman was wearing thin. "So, what happens now in your game plan, Hari?" He whispered.

"Well, I don't expect to move in with you but I would like some hot sex now and then if you don't mind. You have set me on fire, you know, Luc. I was going mad with desire. It was affecting my work, my thoughts. I just had to do something. But it can be a one off if I have offended you, even if I would regret that immensely."

"Do I look as if I am offended?" Luc growled.

"No you look satisfied and so cute!" she giggled.

"Less of the cute! Also I am not sure about the satisfied either. Do you think we could do that again, but this time more slowly?"

"Well, I have all night, so take all the time you want!" she complied.

Chapter Fifteen

Hari awoke the next morning to find herself curled up against a warm male body. Remembering her actions of the previous evening, she ought to have felt ashamed, but instead she felt proud of herself. In her defence, she argued that it was all Luc's fault for being so sexy and tantalising. She was only human after all. She definitely had no regrets and looking at the broad smile that lit up his face on seeing her in his bed she doubted he had any either.

"Bonjour, mon ange!" he whispered against her hair, pulling her into his embrace for a deeply satisfying kiss. "What a lovely way to start the day!"

"I can think of something a little more satisfying if you are game, Cariad!" she replied huskily, rolling on top of him.

"Two minds with but one thought!" he replied joining in the challenge.

So, a new pattern shaped their mornings. Luc found that he enjoyed sharing his bed with his Welsh temptress, so Hari invariably spent the night with him. Their morning showers were often taken together thus prolonging their morning routine. Luc found he didn't mind missing out on his morning workout in the gym as he was doing a far more enjoyable workout. Breakfast was a shared occasion, each contributing something and then it was down to work.

While Luc retired to his recording studio, Hari worked through the admin, updating his schedule, confirming bookings and answering his mail. Then she planned and prepared meals for them to share or to freeze for future use. While she was cooking, Hari invariably listened to her iPod, singing along to her favourite tunes and often dancing around the kitchen. She was literally bubbling over with happiness. Luc was such a lovely man and a great lover; she did not want to tempt fate by pushing her luck and declaring her very deep feelings for him. She would be grateful for their present harmonious relationship and not think about anything deeper or more lasting.

Luc realised he was extremely happy. With the sexual tension gone between them, he found that he had never felt more relaxed and at ease with any other woman. Hari had quietly slipped into his life and she fitted so perfectly that he was surprised at how short a time he had actually known her. She added a new dimension to his life and he found himself looking forward to sharing new experiences with her. He could not wait for their week in Paris—he would make sure it was really special and not just work!

Listening to his new recordings, he also thought that his voice had never sounded better. He was enjoying singing this new genre of music—pop era some people called it. It was actually quite fun! The duets album should also be fun to record. Maybe he would branch out more, like his friend Jason Greene.

Taking a break, Luc went to the kitchen only to find Hari dancing and singing while chopping up vegetables. How did she do that without cutting herself, he marvelled! She was so engrossed in her own little world that she didn't hear him behind her and was startled to find herself wrapped in a manly hug. Turning to face him, her smile was so bright that it warmed him to the core.

"Oh, sorry, Cariad—I didn't see you there! Have you finished? Want a bite to eat?"

"I can think of someone I would like to eat," he growled, kissing her with enthusiasm.

"Mm! What on earth will you friend Mr Greene think if you carry on like this, Mr Wenger?"

"He will be extremely envious of me, Mrs Morgan. Maybe we should get more of this loving out of our system before he arrives. What do you say that we finish early for today and have some fun!" he winked at her.

"Well, if you think that another 24 hours of passionate love will help you to behave when he arrives, let's do it!" she replied.

"Oh, I don't think it will be nearly enough."

"Seriously though, Cariad. How do you want to play this when Mr Greene is here? Shall I sleep in my room? Do you want to keep our relationship private? I don't mind if you do!"

"Oh, I doubt if we are that good actors, Liebchen! It will be pretty obvious that we are involved. I shall let you decide as you are still legally married and I don't want to compromise you. Are you ready to go public?"

"My marriage was over when Rhodri cheated on me! I should never have married him; I realise that now. Do you know that you are only the second man I have ever slept with? I hope you don't think I make a habit of seducing good-looking men. I was so nervous that you would refuse me, cariad. Personally, I am not ashamed of our relationship and I don't mind if we make it public. People will think it anyway, won't they?"

"Agreed! You might as well cancel those second hotel rooms then," he grinned at her. "We won't be needing them!"

Chapter Sixteen

Jason Greene was an extremely good looking American. Tall and dark haired, his chocolate-coloured eyes were warm and friendly. Hari felt relaxed in his company and responded well to his easy manner. He, in turn, was charmed by the enchanting red-head with the lovely green eyes. While Luc was pleased to see them get on well together, he nevertheless felt pangs of jealousy at their easy camaraderie. Surely Hari was not flirting with the American? Was she just being friendly? Why was he feeling so insecure anyway?

"Say what kind of a name is Hari anyway?" Jason was quizzing Hari.

"It is short for Angharad—it's Welsh, see!"

"Oh, that's what your lovely accent is! It sure is captivating—I could listen to you all day. It has a lilt to it— say, do you sing?" He asked.

"Is the Pope Catholic?" She quipped. "I am Welsh, aren't I?"

"Why don't we sing a duet together? Wait, we could even record it! What do you say, Luc?"

"Well, I am sure that Hari is too busy for that!" he grumbled, feeling out of sorts at the very notion. He was cross with himself that he had not thought of it first. After all, he had heard what a sweet voice Hari had. He suddenly realised how important it was to him that they should sing together.

But Jason was not going to be put off that easily. He appealed directly to Hari. Seeing how cross Luc looked, she gave a non-committal reply hoping that there would not be enough time during Jason's brief visit.

Hari deliberately kept out of the way for much of the visit. Jason was a really nice guy and she was flattered by his attention—after all, what woman wouldn't be. He was young, single, and attractive and he obviously liked her. But Luc had her heart. So while she was friendly and hospitable she resisted any overtures by Jason to get to know her better.

"Say, Hari, are you and Luc together?" He finally asked, a little bemused as to why his charms were not working on this enchanting creature. Seeing her discomfort he added, "Ah, that's the way it is! Does he know that you are in love with him?"

Hari looked shocked! "I don't know what you mean?"

"Aw, come on! It's pretty obvious! So, does he know?"

"No! It's not like that, really! We are just good friends!" she protested. "Luc doesn't want a serious relationship. Anyway, this works for us!"

"Don't worry, I won't say anything. But he sure is one hell of a lucky guy. If ever you tire of him call me, won't you?"

"That's really lovely of you, Jason. But that is unlikely to happen."

Although Luc usually enjoyed time spent with Jason—their friendship went back years, he was relieved when the visit ended. They had recorded a couple of songs which they were both pleased with, but were unsure which to include on the album. Luc had been surprised by feeling jealous of Jason's obvious attraction to Hari. Not usually prone to jealousy, his reaction caught him off guard. Berating himself for a fool and understanding that there was no commitment between them did nothing to relieve his annoyance.

Hari picked up on Luc's mood. She was aware of his annoyance at the way Jason flirted with her and did her best not to appear interested. Jason was a lovely man, and had her heart not been already taken she might have been interested. But she was completely smitten with Luc and was finding it hard not to reveal her true feelings—he had warned her about his previous assistant wanting more of him than he was prepared to give. She was determined not to fall into that trap and was grateful for what they had got. It would have to be enough!

Back to their usual routine, life fell into a comfortable pattern for Luc. He had never felt so good—his music was going well, his business was really well organised as Hari proved to be a very efficient assistant, he had never been better fed and his sex life was amazing. Life was good! He just hoped that Hari felt the same way.

He was coming to rely on her more and more, even involving her in his music choice. She had provided him with a list of popular duets to consider and had also slipped in a list of some of her favourite songs which had made him smile. Knowing that her birthday fell at the beginning of March, he had resolved to make her a special recording of these songs as a personal present.

Feeling unsure about some of his song selections, Luc invited Hari to join him in the recording studio so that she could listen and advise. He was amused to see how excited she was to see this side of this job.

"What are all those dials?" She queried walking around the room. "Come, I will show you everything. This is where I record—into this microphone here. Those dials are all tape decks which I will play with when listening to the recording to adjust the sound and tone. Then, I can cut a disc with the finished recording. It's great fun! Listen, after you help me with my song choice, why don't you have a go yourself? You can cut your own disc!"

Hari's eyes grew large with excitement and a huge smile lit up her face, "Oh, do you think I can do that? That would be absolutely magic, Luc! I would love to have a go—but I won't know what to sing!"

"Don't worry about that now—I have got a library of songs for you to choose from with all the lyrics. You will probably take some time choosing one you really like and that suits your range. Now, don't worry about it, will you? It's just an idea," he added seeing how anxious she was looking.

"Right, let's listen to your songs then, and I will give you my honest opinion," she replied, relieved to change the subject. Suddenly, recording herself seemed daunting rather than fun.

Luc instructed Hari to put on a set of headphones as he selected the tracks he wanted her to hear. As he worked, he explained how things were proceeding to Hari. She would listen to six tracks, some he had recorded live himself and others where he had added his voice to a known record, such as *Fields of Gold* sung by the late Eva Cassidy, and *Over the Rainbow* with Mireille Matthieu. With Jason, he duetted *Bring him Home*, and *Morning has Broken*. He duetted *The*

Prayer with his friend Celine Dion and he sang *Hallelujah* solo, trying to decide whom he could duet this track with. He provisionally had Susan Boyle lined up to duet her now famous *I Dreamed a Dream* track. He finished by saying that he would need to put together between ten and twelve tracks altogether, but he was generally pleased with how the album was going.

Luc donned his own earphones before selecting play. When the music started Hari was transported to another world. Listening to Luc's voice through the headphones seemed so intimate—it felt like he was inside her head. His voice was sublime, like smooth caramel. She felt goosebumps all over her body. She was finding it difficult to concentrate on the task as his voice wrapped around her and hypnotised her. Without realising it, tears of emotion were running down her face at his solo rendition of *Hallelujah*. It was so beautiful! But what nearly pushed her over the edge was the duet with Jason *Bring Him Home* which always brought a lump to her throat with its significance to the armed forces.

Seeing her emotional reaction to his songs, Luc quietly passed Hari a large hanky. He guessed that her reaction was a good sign but he would find out when they discussed the tracks.

When the music finally ended, Luc switched off the machine and removed his headphones. Hari still hadn't moved, so he reached across and removed her headphones, too.

He asked her gently, giving her time to compose herself, "Well, what do you think?" He joked, "Not that bad, was it?" attempting to raise a smile from her.

143

"Oh, Luc, or should I call you Sebastien, that was so moving. Your voice! I felt it deep inside me. It is so beautiful, Cariad—I had no idea! It is so different listening to your voice like this—you were inside my head, you were everywhere. I feel totally overwhelmed. I mean I know your voice is beautiful, I have heard you sing before, but not like this! It sent shivers right through me!"

"Does that mean you liked it, then?" He smiled at her enthusiasm, inordinately pleased at her reaction.

"I loved it! Haven't you been listening?" She sighed exasperated.

"Okay I got the message! Right, well which tracks do you think I should include on the album?" He asked.

"All of them! I loved them all!"

"What about *Hallelujah*? At the moment, it is a solo—I will need to find someone to duet with. Any ideas?"

"Why don't you ask your agent for suggestions? Or why don't you send out invites—send out the track and ask people to record their voices on to it—like you did on the Eva Cassidy, which I absolutely adored, by the way!"

"That's a good idea! Let's do that. Right, all I have to do now is select a further five or six tracks. But I am pleased with how it is going. I must say, I am really enjoying this crossover from opera. It is a whole new genre for me. Now then, Liebchen, shall we select a song for you."

Hari was suddenly very nervous about singing in front of Luc. She had selected one of her favourite songs but knew she was too self-conscious to sing it. Seeing her discomfort, Luc suggested that he showed her how to operate the equipment and then he would go and make coffee for them both while she recorded by herself. He explained how the red light came on when someone was recording so that he would not be able to interrupt her.

He gave Hari plenty of time before he returned with a tray of drinks. He was relieved to see that the red light was switched off and wondered how she had managed and if she had enjoyed the experience.

Hari was sitting perched at the edge of her chair waiting for Luc to show her what to do next. She smiled nervously at him, saying:

"Well, I did it! At least I think I did. I haven't dared touch anything in case I do something wrong."

"Why don't you help yourself to coffee and I will check the recording?" He said.

Suddenly, the room was filled with the shy, sweet tones of a very nervous Hari singing *The First Time Ever I Saw Your Face*. Though far from perfect, it was nevertheless achingly beautiful. Seeing her anxious look, Luc caught her up in an embrace, "Ach, mein, Liebchen, das war wunderbar, echt wunderbar!" he was too stunned to speak English.

"Oh, do you really like it? I sound so nervous though!"

"Yes, but that was only your first attempt. You will see that with a little practise your voice will become stronger. You just need practise and some confidence! Come, I will teach you!"

Several hours later, Hari was exhausted and her voice was nearly hoarse through overuse. Luc encouraged her to gargle and taught her some voice exercises to help her relax her voice box. He also showed her how to use her diaphragm to project her voice without straining it. Then he insisted that they take a break. He suggested a swim and a sauna and no more singing for today. He added that they would have another attempt tomorrow and emphasised that it should be an enjoyable experience or it would show in her vocals.

The next day after their usual office time checking the mail and updating the calendar, Hari left Luc to talk with his agent and went down to the recording studio to have a second attempt at the song. She felt less nervous this time and remembered to do the breathing exercises that Luc had shown her. She also stood taller using her diaphragm to help project her voice. This time, it felt better—she sang more easily and with greater confidence. She was actually looking forward to hearing it back, but thought she should wait until Luc returned. Having time to kill, she tentatively sought out the lyrics for *Hallelujah* and decided to record that too. It was one of her favourites but she would never have thought to sing it. To her surprise, it fitted well into her range and she sang it with relative ease. Just as she finished recording, Luc entered the room, buoyant from his phone call. Apparently, his agent had several people lined up for his duet album he was pleased to report.

"Now then, mein, Liebchen, let us hear version number two. How did it go? Did you feel better?"

"I think it went really well. I followed your instructions about breathing and how I stand and my voice certainly felt stronger. Tell me what you think," she added looking hopeful.

Hari didn't need Luc to say anything about this recording as his smile said it all. He picked her up and swung her round saying, "Yes! Yes! Yes! You did it! That's perfect, mon ange!"

Just then, her sweet voice started singing *Hallelujah*. Luc stood in amazement with Hari still in his arms. He stared into her eyes as he listened to her beautiful rendition of the song.

Who would have thought that she hid this amazing talent? Putting her down, he danced her slowly the room in time to the music singing softly along to the tune. When the music ended, he whispered in her ear, "How erotic was that? I know just what you mean about the music getting deep inside of you. You are amazing. So, I want to make love to you right now, is that wrong?"

"Well, if it is that makes two of us, Cariad. It is quite a turn on this music making, isn't it? I never knew!"

"I don't think I can wait to get you upstairs," he groaned in response. "Just a minute!"

Grabbing some cushions, Luc made a temporary bed on the floor. Before dragging Hari down with him, he put her songs on a loop so that they could make slow sensual love to her lovely voice.

Chapter Seventeen

By the end of the week, Luc had lined up two more artists to duet on his album. He had arranged to meet them both in Rome where he was due the next day for the New Year's concert. Unfortunately, one of the artists was none other than Maria Benedetto who had offered to sing *You Don't Bring me Flowers Anymore* with him. Against his better judgement, Luc was talked into accepting the offer by his agent. After all, she was a crowd winner and would help to sell the album.

Without Hari's knowledge, Luc had sent his agent a copy of Hallelujah where he had blended both their voices. Not revealing to whom the mystery voice belonged, he was interested to get his agent's reaction.

Since, he would need to spend a few more days in Rome to do the extra recordings, Luc had asked Hari to extend their hotel booking for three further nights. He promised her that he would not have to work the whole time and he was looking forward to spending quality time with his lovely lady.

Hari realised just how famous Luc was when they flew first class and were met by a chauffeur-driven limousine. The hotel was the height of luxury and she was told that she had to make full use of all the facilities. There were hordes of fans and autograph hunters everywhere they went. Apparently, the concert was a huge annual event with a plethora of famous artists, some of whom Hari recognised. She was beyond excited!

It was a black-tie event and Luc suggested that Hari wore the gown he had bought her.

She asked incredulously. "How many of these events do you do each year then, Luc?"

"Oh, quite a few!" he smiled his reply. "You will have to buy quite a few more gowns, mein Liebchen! Let's see if we can fit in some shopping time, nein? No expense spared as it is charged to the business," he added.

"Oh, my gosh! I can't believe this is really happening," she squealed, throwing herself onto the enormous bed. "Wow, Luc, I feel like the Princess and the Pea, this bed is huge. I shall need a ladder to climb into it," she giggled.

"Come and join me, lover! Have we time to christen this magnificent piece of furniture?" She purred holding out her arms to him.

Luc did not need a further invitation. Taking a running leap, he landed on top of her, saying, "There is always time for this, Liebling!" and proceeded to divest her of all unnecessary garments.

Lying snuggled in Luc's arms after some wonderful sex, Hari whispered, "Have you seen the ensuite? I think we need to christen that next!"

"Hexe! You are insatiable!" he groaned.

"Only with you, Cariad, I am going to take a lovely bath with a glass of bubbly, truly decadent I am! Join me if you want," she purred seductively, walking with a deliberate wiggle towards the bathroom.

Giving her a head start, Luc stretched out on the bed, with a huge grin on his face. How had he deserved this lovely creature, he wondered? What a lucky guy! He wanted to tell the whole world he was so happy. Just then his phone buzzed—it was his mother telling him that she and Vati had managed to get last minute tickets to the concert and were staying in a nearby hotel. She wished him luck for tonight and arranged to meet up for lunch the next day. Hearing Hari's voice in the background, she smiled secretly to herself and told him to pass on their love to his charming assistant. Who did he think he was fooling with his business relationship!

"What took you so long? I have almost finished this glass of bubbly. I will be quite sozzled soon and incapable of anything," she giggled.

"You better not drink anymore of that," he said, "I need you sober with all your wits about you." So saying, Luc took away the glass and climbed into the bath behind her nestling her in between his legs. "Now, let's see what I can do to sober you up!" he added nuzzling her neck and slowly caressing her body with his hands.

"Oooh, that feels so good. I feel better already," she moaned.

As they were getting dressed later, Luc told Hari about his mother's phone call, saying his parents would be at the concert, too, so she would have company. He added that they would be meeting for lunch the next day and maybe she should arrange to go shopping with Virginie who had an excellent eye for fashion and would know what would be suitable for such occasions.

Helping Luc with his bow tie, Hari could not believe that she was actually dating this gorgeous man. She felt somewhat self-conscious as they walked arm in arm through the hotel, to be met by a chauffeur in reception. Hari wondered if she would ever get used to all this attention and she marvelled at Luc's composure. But then he had grown up in this sort of environment with both his parents being celebrated performers themselves. She fervently hoped that she could live up to his expectations and not come across as gauche.

The concert hall was magnificent. Hari did not have time to take in all its splendour as Luc walked purposefully towards backstage and his own dressing room pulling Hari along in his wake. As he prepared himself for his number which was halfway through the concert, Hari sat quietly in the corner, trying not to fidget. Luc was relieved when his parents called by as he was finding Hari's nervous energy somewhat distracting. She would soon get used to these occasions he told himself.

After exchanging greetings with his parents, Luc gave an excited Hari into their care saying that he had reserved a box. Virginie recognised the nervous tension of an artist before going on to perform and could see that Hari was too much of a distraction. Wishing him luck, she took the rather lovely Welsh woman under her wing, revelling in her obvious enthusiasm. She had a definite glow about her and Virginie wondered whether her son was responsible for it. She very much hoped so.

It was the most amazing concert, a truly magical experience and Hari thought she would never get used to the emotional impact it had on her senses. When Luc came on stage, she sat forward resting her arms on the edge of the box and just drowned in his eyes. He seemed to be singing directly to her, his voice melted her very core. Watching her closely,

Virginie recognised a woman in love—if she was not mistaken seeing her son's performance he was equally smitten, but did he know it?

Chapter Eighteen

Back in the hotel room, Luc was exhausted after his performance. Apart from his solo, he had a duet and also took part in the finale. He had already explained his usual routine to Hari so she was not surprised when he took a long shower before getting into bed and falling asleep immediately. Lying beside him and listening to his rhythmic breathing, Hari relived the magical evening before finally sleeping.

Luc was full of energy the next morning as Hari found on being awakened by his kiss. He ordered breakfast and suggested they made a leisurely morning enjoying the home comforts before meeting his parents for lunch. He was pleased that Virginie had offered to take Hari shopping as this freed him to do some recordings. He was not looking forward to his meeting with Maria but preferred to get it out of the way. He also wondered whether the dinner date would be mentioned or whether she had in fact defaulted.

Lunch with his parents was a relaxed affair. They had got to know Hari well over the holidays and so there was no discomfort between them all. Virginie observed the younger couple closely and discerned a greater intimacy between them. They seem well suited and she hoped that her suspicions were correct. It was time that her charming son settled down and she really liked this lovely Welsh girl with her down to earth attitude. She was like a breath of fresh air.

Luc insisted on paying for lunch and then took his leave, saying he would see Hari back at the hotel. He embraced both his parents thanking them for the visit and promising to meet up again soon.

Dieter excused himself from the shopping trip jokingly telling his wife not to spend too much and kissing Hari fondly.

"Eh bien, ma chère," Virginie addressed Hari, "my charming son has indicated that you need some concert outfits, non?"

"Yes please! I only have the dress he bought me. Luc said I should look for several more like that but he said you would set me right!"

"Alors! J'adore le shopping, especially when I am spending someone else's money. Fortunately, my son has much to spend. So, let us follow his orders and spend!" she grinned wickedly at Hari.

"Oh no! Why don't I like the sound of that?" She replied with a smile.

True to her word, Virginie spent a lot of Luc's money. She had an excellent eye and knew instinctively what suited Hari's build and colouring. She also knew from experience the types of outfits needed for such occasions. Hari had never tried on so many clothes in her life before but with Virginie's encouragement, she actually enjoyed herself. They ended up buying four gowns and two tea dresses plus two elegant pants suits. Virginie also insisted that Hari needed suitable shoes and bags. They compromised on two pairs of court shoes, and a pair of black patent slingbacks. Virginie was amused by the two bags chosen by Hari who insisted that they had to be large enough to hold her invaluable notebook which she always carried with her!

Just when Hari thought they had finished Virginie dragged her into one final department—lingerie! Feeling embarrassed to be looking at underwear with Luc's mother she soon found that no Frenchwoman would be seen dead without luxury silk underclothes. She insisted that Hari bought several sets of matching bra and pants in such flimsy material that Hari thought they were hardly worth wearing! Virginie did not stop there—suspenders and silk stockings, lace teddies and two very glamorous nightdresses and negligée sets were added to the long list. Hari did not dare look at the mounting cost of this shopping expedition—she was so overwhelmed by Virginie's decisive personality that she was literally stunned by how many purchases they had made. What would Luc say? She would offer to pay for some of this but she honestly could not afford it. Her enjoyment was almost ruined by feelings of guilt. Seeing her face, Virginie hastily reassured her that Luc would not be surprised by the amount spent and added wickedly that he would be enjoying seeing her in such lovely clothes, especially the lingerie, non? Hari's blush revealed much about her relationship with Luc and Virginie was pleased to note that she did not deny anything. Eh bien, she was right! Wondering how she was going to get all her purchases back to the hotel, Hari was surprised to watch Virginie organising delivery to Mr Wenger's suite at the Borgo Pio Hotel. Feeling rather like royalty, she then insisted on treating her to dinner in the exclusive restaurant with panoramic views.

"I have had such a lovely day, Virginie, I can't begin to thank you!" she said with her eyes sparkling and a happy smile on her face. "I am exhausted though. I am rather glad that we bought so much now, I won't need to shop again in a while!"

"Mais, non, ma chère! That is not the attitude! You will be in Paris soon—you must make the most of the opportunity to buy some sexy clothes. The French are even better at fashion than the Italians. Bien sûr, but I am biased!" she smiled, tapping Hari gently on the hand. "Men say they are not interested in what women wear, but believe me they appreciate a well turned-out woman. They are all the same when it comes down to the sexy underclothes, non! Besides, once you have tried the luxurious feel of well-made lingerie you will never look back, je t'assure. We women owe it to ourselves to feel good in our own skin, non?"

"I suppose so, but I have never looked at it like that."

"Well, next time we talk, just tell me that I am wrong!" Virginie smiled at her. "Now, then let us choose something naughty to eat, we have earned a treat after all that hard work, non? And then you can tell me how you are getting on with my charming son. I do hope he is not working you too hard?"

By the time Hari returned to the hotel, she knew exactly how it must feel to be grilled by investigators. She had never been any good at subterfuge and Virginie was an expert interviewer who was left in no doubt as to the exact relationship between the young couple. Hari had even told her all about Rhodri and found it reassuring talking about her marriage with someone who had never met her husband. Virginie was compassionate and sympathetic, not passing judgement but listening without comment. She did not need to ask Hari how she felt about her son as it was evident. She just wondered whether this lovely Welsh lady was herself aware that she was in love with Luc. She hoped that Hari would get the divorce she needed so that she could move on with her life, whether that included Luc or not.

Arriving back in reception, Hari was informed that a delivery had been made and taken up to her room. Signor Wenger was still not back she was informed so would la Signora like to dine alone? Hari explained that she had already eaten. Walking into their room Hari was amazed at the amount of parcels which greeted her. She was so overwhelmed by feelings of guilt that she decided not to open any of them in case they needed to be returned. She would treat herself to a long soak in a deep bubble bath with a glass of bubbly! She wondered how late Luc would be? She had not thought to ask him.

After a leisurely soak and two glasses of bubbly, Hari could not keep her eyes open. She had wanted to stay up for Luc to share her day with him but exhaustion overtook her and she fell into a deep sleep not even stirring when he climbed in beside her.

Hari was awakened by a sensual kiss which jerked her into consciousness and then deepened with the promise of something more. Her body responded immediately as she wrapped her arms around Luc's neck. Loving him felt like coming home.

"What a lovely awakening, Cariad," she sighed, replete with loving. She asked nuzzling his neck, "Did you have a good day recording?"

"Productive!" he replied enigmatically. "As I see yours was! Did you leave anything in the shops?" He quipped staring at the mound of packages. Suddenly, Hari was all attention. Sitting up abruptly, she looked anxiously into his face. Trying not to laugh at her expression, Luc adopted a stern face causing her to quickly defend herself.

"Oh, Cariad, I am so sorry. Your mam insisted that I needed all these things. She is a difficult woman to say not to, isn't she? But I haven't unwrapped anything so I can send them back."

She looked so worried that Luc decided not to continue with his pretended annoyance. Instead he caught her into a hug and laughed.

"Don't worry, meine Liebling! If Maman says you need all this then who am I to argue. Perhaps we had better have a shower and breakfast before you do your fashion show for me. I am quite looking forward to my private viewing." Hari blushed at the thought of some of the items she had bought. Then berated herself since he would be seeing them all soon anyway. She was suddenly embarrassed that he should see some of the more intimate clothing that Virginie had chosen. She realised what a world of difference existed between the Wengers and the Prices. Her mam would never think to wear such glamorous clothes. Hari felt herself trapped between two worlds and felt very unsure of her role.

Having lingered over breakfast for as long as possible, the moment came when Hari could not delay opening the parcels any longer. Luc made himself comfortable in an armchair dressed only in a towelling dressing gown and poured himself a cup of coffee.

"Well then, let us see what you have been spending my money on then, meine Liebling!" he said with an encouraging smile on his face.

"Shall I change in the bathroom to give you a better effect?" She suggested.

"There is no need. Besides, you may want a hand with the zippers. Are you shy, Liebchen?" He asked tenderly.

"Just a little, it seems odd to be dressing and undressing in front of you like this. I am not comfortable really!"

"Well, then please use the bathroom or else I shall turn my back and look out of the window. You can tell me when you are ready—would that be easier?"

"Yes please, if you don't mind. I know I am being silly, but I am feeling a bit out of my depth suddenly."

"Don't worry, Liebchen! You do not have to keep anything you are uncomfortable about. Maman was being helpful but she can be rather overwhelming. Now, I shall turn my back and admire this lovely view of Rome. Take your time."

Hari was too nervous to try on the new underclothes, so she found some of her own and selected one of the new gowns. It was a deep wine-coloured velvet sheath dress with a fan tail. She had to wear heels with this so chose the black patent slingbacks which were her favourite.

"You can look now," she said shyly.

Luc turned around and the look on his face told her he approved. "You look beautiful, Liebchen! That colour goes well with your gorgeous hair. Do you like it? Does it feel comfortable?"

"Yes! It is not too tight, is it?"

"Not in my eyes. You look lovely! I think that is a keeper, don't you? So, the next one."

An hour later, Hari had tried on all the outfits. Luc could not find fault with a single item—his mother had exquisite taste as he had always known. When he enquired after the remaining packages, Hari said they were undergarments but she was not sure about them. They seemed too glamorous, so not her! She was sure she would never wear them and was thinking of returning them. "Let me see! No, you don't have to try them on for me if you feel uncomfortable."

He opened some of the packages and Hari could tell from his reaction that he liked what he saw.

"Oh my! Would you look at these? Such lovely silk—I bet it feels lovely against the skin! Are you sure you wouldn't like to try one set on? For me?" He asked with a slow smile. "Mind you how on earth would I be able to concentrate on singing if I am imagining you wearing such sexy clothes?"

"See! That's what I mean! How can I wear something so obviously sexy? I would feel like everyone could see through my clothes."

"But in fact the only one who would see you like that is yourself and me if I am lucky. Doesn't every woman want to wear silk? What is wrong with feeling sensuous? As a Frenchwoman, Maman believes that what you wear under your clothes is equally important. She says that exotic silk underwear gives her confidence in herself as a woman. Try them on, Liebchen, just one set. If you don't love them, the rest can be returned."

"Alright then! Your mam did say that the outfits would be improved by wearing the correct underwear. I suppose she knows what she is talking about." Luc was about to turn around but Hari said she was going to change in the bathroom. A short while later, she opened the door and stood shyly in the entrance. Luc turned on hearing the door open. His breath caught in his throat and he felt his pulse race at the sight of Hari in sexy silk underwear, holding out his arms to her, he called her over to him. Shyly, Hari approached and was pulled down onto his lap.

"Oh, meine Liebling, du bist so schön! I am going to have such fun removing these underclothes!" he whispered, nuzzling her neck while his hands caressed the silk material making Hari shudder with longing.

"Bachgen drwg!" she replied throatily.

When his eyebrows queried this phrase, she translated, "Bad Boy!" to which he replied, "oh, I do hope so!" and picking her up he carried her over to the bed.

"Luc what if we are disturbed?"

"Don't worry, Schätzchen. I put a do not disturb sign on the door while you were trying on the clothes. Now, let me see how these work?" He whispered to a giggling Hari. Maybe she would keep the underwear after all!

By the time Luc and Hari had given a verdict on all the clothing, it was early afternoon. Despite her best intentions, nothing was being returned! She had to admit that Virginie knew what she was talking about. From Luc's obvious enjoyment, he felt it was money well spent.

Ordering room service yet again, Luc decided to explain to Hari just how unglamorous his life really was. Sure he travelled the world, went to exotic places, but he rarely saw more than the inside of his hotel room and the concert hall. If he tried to sightsee, he was mobbed by frantic fans who wanted to tear at his clothes. He was followed everywhere if word of his whereabouts spread. That is why he had a chauffeur-driven limousine everywhere and the hotels were carefully chosen to give him the maximum privacy.

When Hari had first seen his opulent home, she was critical of the expense spent finding it ostentatious in the extreme. Luc explained that it was in fact a fortress designed to keep his life private. The same applied to his cars with their blackened-out windows—all chosen for privacy. Rather than glamorous, his life was in fact rather lonely. So, he was delighted to be able to share his imprisonment with her, he laughed.

Hari suddenly felt sorry for this lovely man. She had never really taken the time to understand his life but had been rather critical of his expensive lifestyle in her ignorance. She never realised how lonely a life on tour could be. If her company helped to alleviate Luc's loneliness on his tours, then she could only be glad, especially if it went some way to putting off the female fans keen on getting close to him.

Returning their empty plates to the trolley, Hari noticed a newspaper with Luc's photo on the front page. She went over to pick it up and saw a photo of Luc being kissed by Maria Benedetto. Intrigued, she read the accompanying article in which Maria hinted at a renewed relationship between herself and Luc. "What have you got there?" Luc queried, seeing Hari absorbed in a newspaper article.

"Oh, just something about you and Maria—apparently you are an item!"

"What! Let me see! Quatsch! She really is a dreadful woman!" he moaned.

"Want to tell me about it?" Hari asked, seemingly unconcerned.

"There is nothing to tell! We worked on our duet together which went well despite Maria insisting that we need to do further recordings today. Then she informed me that she had booked a table for us at her hotel. Apparently, this was from the auction. What she did not say was that she had arranged for a photographer to be there with a journalist. She was literally all over me implying that we had an intimate relationship. At the end of the meal, she tried to entice me upstairs to her room saying she had a present for me. Well, I ran for it, I can tell you! That woman is trouble!"

"So, you are not seeing her privately?" Hari asked innocently, looking at Luc from under her eyebrows.

"How can you even ask that?" He started to defend himself when he saw the smile on her face. "Oh, you! You had me going for a moment, there! I thought you were serious."

"Ah, Cariad, it was worth it to see the look of horror on your face. Is she really so scary?"

"Worse—a real man eater! Gosh, Hari, you had me going there! I hope you know me better than that to even think I could two time you. I am strictly a one-woman man, always! You are woman enough for me."

"I am glad to hear it as I don't share at all!" she muttered fiercely, probably remembering Rhodri's betrayal of their marriage vows.

"Come here, Liebchen, and let me show how I feel about you!" he whispered seductively into her ear and running his hands down her body.

Hari groaned throatily feeling her body respond instantly to his touch. What she loved about Luc was his ability to make her laugh, the way he listened to her and cared about her opinions, but mostly how he made her body ignite with passion at his merest touch. She felt a complete woman in his arms.

Chapter Nineteen

When they returned to Gstaad, Hari looked at Luc's home with fresh eyes. After their conversation, she could see how it was like a fortress despite all its luxuries. If it weren't for her presence, he would be almost completely alone. She wondered whether it would be better for Luc if she found him a cook. With only a part-time cleaner and gardener, his contact with the outside world was limited. She put the question to Luc once they were unpacked. He listened to her argument and said that although he was quite happy with the current arrangement if Hari wanted to change things, he would follow her guidance. He added that it seemed unfair of him to expect her to be both his assistant and his cook, and that the lack of social contact could equally be applied to Hari herself. When had she last gone out?

Hari argued that she loved cooking and didn't mind taking on both roles. As for a social life, she had her skiing lessons. Besides she really didn't know anyone in Gstaad.

"So, Liebchen, despite your protests about our insular lifestyle, you don't want to change anything?" He stated with a bemused smile.

"Bonkers, aren't I?" She quipped.

"Bonkers? What a strange word!"

"Doof in your language!"

Luc burst out laughing. What a little conundrum she was!

"Right, then, glad we got that out of the way! So how about some lunch?" She said with a smile, leading the way into the kitchen. "Welsh Rarebit, do you, Cariad?"

Luc was so glad to be back home with this lovely Welsh lady organising his life. He realised how happy she made him, how much he took her presence for granted. He couldn't remember a time when she wasn't there yet it had only been a few short months.

They quickly got back into an efficient work routine. Once the mail had been sorted and actioned, Hari spent time updating the diary and wall chart, then organised all her phone calls setting up meetings for Luc and arranging recordings with other artists. When Luc had managed his personal mail and phone calls, he went down to his recording studio to finalise the songs on his duets album, leaving Hari free.

Checking the food store, Hari decided that she needed to do a supermarket trip. She sat down with a coffee and planned several meals, simultaneously writing a long shopping trip. Leaving a note for Luc, as she wouldn't interrupt his recording session, she selected the smallest car from the garage and set off for town.

Since, she had not had a lot of practice driving abroad, Hari concentrated very hard on the road, so was unaware of being photographed as she exited the property. She took her time shopping getting extra items that weren't on her list. Putting all the bags in the boot of her car, she decided to have a look around for some birthday present ideas. She shared a March birthday with her mother and wanted to find her something special, so was looking for inspiration.

She was in the stationers looking for a suitable card when she caught sight of herself on the front page of a newspaper. Rushing over to see what it was all about she was horrified to see an article about her marriage. Quickly buying a copy, she took the paper outside to read. With shaking hands, she read that her in-laws had talked extensively to a journalist berating her for deserting their son, who was heartbroken. They explained that Hari and Rhodri had been childhood sweethearts, inseparable, and they were devastated that she had walked out on her marriage and was living with this Swiss celebrity. She had her head turned by fame and wealth and had turned her back on her roots. But she would be forgiven if she came home. Their son was an honourable man, an army officer, who was missing his wife and just wanted her back. They all hoped that she would come to her senses. She had obviously been seduced by this Sebastien fellow! A wedding photo and another of Hari and Rhodri in younger, happier days were attached to the article.

Hari was livid. How dare they slander Luc in this way! They were making her out to be an adulteress! She was shaking so much she couldn't move. Suddenly, her phone buzzed. It was Luc! She couldn't talk to him right now she was too upset. It went through to message. She had apparently been gone for several hours and he was just checking she was okay driving his car, knowing how nervous she was.

Hari was in a dilemma. She mustn't talk to Luc until she had calmed down but she was too upset to drive. She decided to have a cup of coffee to calm her nerves and then decide. She texted Luc to say she was card shopping and would be home soon.

After two strong cups of coffee, Hari had stopped shaking. For the first time since meeting Luc, she understood what he meant about the lack of privacy. She felt as if she was being watched, her skin prickling with tension. She felt sick and just wanted to be safely back home with Luc. But she had no idea how she was going to manage the drive feeling so uptight. Knowing that she could not remain in the cafe forever, Hari reluctantly made a move. She almost ran to the car and once inside she locked all the doors. Not daring to look around and feeling quite paranoid, she carefully drove home. She had never been more thankful to turn into the gated entrance and once the gates closed behind her she drove into the garage. Switching off the engine Hari found she could not move; her whole body was rigid with tension.

This was how Luc found her sometime later. He had seen her car turn in at the gates on the video camera and went down to help carry the shopping. Seeing Hari unmoving at the wheel Luc rushed to open the driver's door.

"Hari, was ist los? Are you hurt?" His heart almost stopped to see the anguished look on her face. Her body was absolutely rigid as if she was holding herself together with a huge effort. Getting no response from her, Luc was seriously worried. He gently took hold of her arm and edged her out of the car. Picking her up, he carried her into the house. Setting her down on the sofa Luc knelt down in front of her and started rubbing her hands talking softly to her.

"Hari, Liebchen! Please tell me what happened?"

She shook her head from side to side, moaning softly; "Oh, how could they? Oh, Luc, I am so sorry!" she sighed, bursting into tears.

Sitting down next to her, Luc pulled her onto his lap and cuddled her hard against him, stroking her hair and whispering softly to reassure her that everything would be alright. Gradually, the crying lessened and an exhausted Hari went to freshen up, still refusing to tell Luc what had happened.

When she finally returned, red eyed and emotional, she told him to fetch the newspaper from the car. While Luc did just that Hari sat on the sofa with her head in her hands wondering what on earth she was going to do. She should resign! But there was no way that she was ever going back to Wales with those evil people spreading lies about this wonderful man who had rescued her on more than one occasion and who had given her back her self-respect. She cared less about the lies aimed at her, but Luc did not deserve any of those comments. How unfair life was! Just because he was famous he became a target for all sorts of scurrilous gossip.

Luc was still reading the article when he finally reappeared. His face was furious, "How dare they say such hateful things about you, Hari? It is beyond belief! My, poor darling, no wonder you were in such a state. Why didn't you call me? How on earth did you manage to drive after reading that rubbish! I shall sue the paper," he ranted angrily.

Hari almost laughed at his outrage on her behalf. How like him to jump to her defence like a knight in shining armour ready to defend his lady.

"But, Luc, what about those awful things they said about you? How dare they? They don't even know you—they have never met you! I am absolutely livid I could hit someone!" she growled angrily.

"Come, Schätzen! Let's put things in perspective! You are still married and we are in a relationship. Those are the facts. People will put their own spin on things especially if it sells papers. At the end of the day, no one is really hurt apart from our feelings. I personally don't care what people say as long as I have you. Now, what say we unload the shopping and have something nice to eat and a stiff drink. Ok, mein Liebchen?" He pulled her gently into his arms and kissed her softly on the lips, then giving her bottom a little tap he said: "Come!"

Still smarting with anger, nevertheless Hari followed Luc's lead. They worked closely together putting away the shopping, then preparing the meal. A glass or two of wine helped to dull her pain and with soft music playing in the background Hari gradually felt herself relaxing.

"I was going to suggest a workout with the punch ball and then a swim, but I think maybe you are a little tipsy, kleine!" suggested Luc. "I would not want you to drown!"

"You would rescue me, my Sir Galahad!" slurred Hari, draping her arms around his neck and nuzzling him. "You are always rescuing me! I don't deserve you—all I have brought you is trouble!" she moaned.

"Ridiculous! You have brought me joy and laughter and companionship and so much more, I can't even begin to count the ways you have enriched my life. If you need rescuing, I hope I am always there to rescue you!" he added tenderly.

"What am I going to do about the Morgans? How can I ever go home again after that defamation?"

"Sshh. Don't worry, Liebchen. When the time comes, I will be there to hold your hand. You will not face this alone. You are no longer alone! Besides, I am sure your family will not take these lies easily. Your Mutter knows the truth, nicht wahr? She will defend her little one like a fierce lioness, never fear!"

Hari realised that what Luc said was true. Her parents would be furious and there would no doubt be a deep rift between the families for the first time in years. Since her family outnumbered the Morgans she had a lot of support. Trying not to read too much into Luc's declaration that he would be beside her when she confronted her in-laws, Hari was nevertheless heartened by his total support. Deciding that Hari probably needed some sleep rather than more wine, Luc quickly picked her up before she could protest and carried her up to her bedroom. When he placed her gently on the bed, she refused to remove her arms from around his neck and pulled him down on top of her.

"You are going nowhere, lover!" she giggled, nuzzling his neck.

"I think maybe you have had a little too much to drink, mein Liebchen!" Luc said, kissing her tenderly.

"Maybe, but I am not incapable, and would like a little loving, pretty please!" she murmured throatily against his ear. "If you have forgotten how, let me show you," she giggled, undoing his shirt.

"Yes, I think maybe I have forgotten what to do, Schätzen!" he smiled into her eyes. "Could you show me?"

"Well, I am a teacher after all!" she giggled and proceeded to show Luc exactly how she liked to be loved.

Chapter Twenty

When Hari switched on her phone the next morning, there were several missed phone calls from almost every member of her family. She really did not want to talk to anyone so she decided to do nothing about them.

While they were in the kitchen eating breakfast, her phone rang. It was her mother. She really was not in the right frame of mind to talk to her right now, so she let it go to message. It rang again and again, until Luc suggested that she should take it! If not, he would! When it rang again Hari reluctantly answered. "Hello, Mam. Yes, I have seen the article and I really don't want to talk about it right now."

"But, Cariad, it was all a mistake," interrupted Mrs Price. "They were tricked into it. Bryn was down the pub and a bit worse for wear when this chap kept asking him questions. He was a bit indiscreet but he never said half of what was reported, Cariad. The Morgans are devastated and wanted to ring you to explain but knew you would not want to talk to them."

Hari asked bitterly, "How did they get the photos, Mam?"

"Well now, Cariad. A lady journalist turned up at their house but Mari refused to talk to her. Apparently, the lady was taken ill and asked for a glass of water. When Mari's back was turned, she must have taken snaps of those photos. You know how Mari has them on show in their front room. If you look closely, you can tell they are images taken through a frame—they are not clear. Honest, Cariad, Mari and Bryn are beside themselves. They love you, Cariad. Of course, they are hurting that you and Rhodri have split up and are desperate for you to patch things up, but they would never betray you like this. Think about it, Cariad! They are not nasty people. They were simply fooled by crafty journalists. There should be a law against it, so there should!" Mrs Price complained angrily.

Hari listened to her mother's explanation and realised that there was a lot of truth in what she said.

"Hari, Cariad, I know this has hurt you deeply but don't let some stupid journalists get the better of you! Rise above it. You know in your heart that the Morgans were not to blame. Please, Cariad, don't let this spoil how we all are together. I couldn't bear to lose you!" With that Mrs Price started sobbing. Hari could not stand hearing her mother cry.

"Oh, Mam, don't get upset," she said shakily. "Yes, it hurt me deeply. Of course, I thought it was in revenge for leaving Rhodri. But I agree with you that they are not spiteful people, just hurting like all of us. Oh, Mam, why does life have to be so cruel? Why does my leaving Rhodri hurt so many people? Oh, the stupid man! Why couldn't he have kept his prick in his pants!" she exploded with indignation.

This had the desired effect on Mrs Price who stopped crying to remonstrate with her daughter for her unladylike language.

"Sorry, Mam, I just get so angry at being used like this. First, Rhodri, now strangers having a go. What rights have they anyway! Do you know what hurts me the most? That Luc has been dragged into this. He has been nothing but kindness itself and the names they are calling him. Shameful, it is! I wouldn't blame him if he sacked me, then where would I be? I have no money as Rhodri is refusing to act the gentleman even though he knows I will never take him back."

"But, Cariad, you could always come home. Look for a job here. We would support you until then."

"Mam, I know you would. Diolch yn fawr! But I cannot come home yet. I need to get things sorted first and I need to be stronger to face everyone."

"But, Cariad, what about your birthday? Won't we be seeing you?"

"Leave it with me, Mam, but I would like you and Dad to come out here on a visit. A joint birthday present, like. I will send you the money for your fare and sort out accommodation. Would you like that?"

"Oh, Cariad, are you sure? That would be lovely! Oh, what on earth should I wear?"

Hari was pleased to hear the excitement in her mother's voice. Somehow she would arrange this visit. It was important to her. Promising her mother that she would be in touch soon, and ensuring her that she was feeling better about the newspaper article, she asked her to tell the Morgans she understood and they were not at fault.

Once, the call had ended, Hari sat for a long time in a bemused state. The conversation with her mother had thrown up a lot of questions. She considered how close the two families were. Her mother was correct in saying that the Morgans had always been like family to her, which is probably why she drifted into marriage with Rhodri.

Everyone expected it! They didn't really have much option, did they? It was a done deal between the families, she realised. For the first time, Hari saw things from Rhodri's point of view. Had he actually wanted to marry her? Did he feel pressured into it? Maybe he didn't love her that way, and that led to his affairs. She wasn't condoning his behaviour but maybe there was a reason behind it.

When Luc finally came to find her, having given her space to handle the difficult phone call, he was met with a very pensive Hari.

"Also, mein Liebchen, ist alles gut?" He asked tentatively, sitting beside her and gently putting his arm around her.

"Better, thanks. It wasn't a deliberate plot to besmirch my character—they were tricked! Wretched journalists! There should be a law against them!" she added angrily.

"I am glad that things have been resolved, mein Liebchen. I do not like to see you hurting like that! But what are you thinking about so deeply?"

Hari explained her new insight into her marriage. Maybe Rhodri didn't love her enough? Maybe he saw her more as a friend?

Luc argued that whether or not that was true, he had taken marriage vows and he should have honoured them. How he treated Hari was disrespectful. If the marriage was a mistake, he should have been honest enough to talk about it and come to an agreement between them.

Hari agreed with everything Luc said. That was her reaction, too. Nothing condoned Rhodri's betrayal. That was what hurt her the most while undermining her self-confidence and making her feel less of a woman.

"Right!" said Luc. "We are going out. We are going shopping and then to a restaurant. We are going to make a very public display of ourselves and not hide away like criminals," he stated forcefully. "Go and make yourself look glamorous so no one can miss you. We shall leave in half an hour!"

Once in the car, Luc asked Hari if there was anything she wanted to buy. She suddenly remembered how the dreadful newspaper article had put all thoughts of buying a present for her mother out of her mind. She told Luc about this, and then added that she had thought of the ideal present. She was going to pay for her parents to visit her in Gstaad. Could he recommend a nice hotel, nothing too posh as they would be uncomfortable?

"But, Liebchen, they must stay with us. There is plenty of room. I would love to meet them, too. Or would you rather not?" He asked anxiously, not entirely sure how Hari viewed their private relationship.

"Are you sure, Luc? That is so kind of you! I would love that," she replied enthusiastically.

"Would you prefer to keep our relationship strictly business-like during their visit?" Luc added. "I would quite understand if you did."

"I am not sure. I am not ashamed of being with you. But it might be awkward. On the other hand, I am not sure I could keep my distance," she added with a cheeky grin, "you have cast quite a spell over me, Herr Wenger!"

"As you have on me, meine Hexe! Well, let's not make that decision at the moment, but please pass on the invitation to your parents. So, what shall we shop for? I know! Don't you have a birthday coming up soon? Let me buy you a present—anything you like within reason," he added with a big grin.

Hari asked astonished, "How did you know about my birthday?"

"Aha! I have my ways, you know!" he chortled.

She asked in return, "When is your birthday, then?"

"That is for me to know and for you to find out!" he teased.

"Well, I shall have to tickle it out of you later," she suggested wickedly.

"Oh, please no! Not the tickles! Anything, but that!" he quipped. Soon, they were both laughing so much their sides hurt.

They arrived at the centre in a relaxed, happy mood, still giggling uncontrollably. Not bothering to attempt any disguise, Luc dragged Hari around all the shops trying to tempt her into buying all sorts of things. At the same time, he watched her carefully to see what especially took her interest. He took her to several jewellery shops so that he could find out her taste—did she prefer gold, white gold or silver? Was she a bracelet lover? Did she like modern or antique? What was her favourite stone? He made a mental note of everything planning to return by himself. He would also consult his mother and maybe even Mrs Price, once he had met her.

Thinking of his mother, Luc decided that it was time he invited his parents on a visit. He especially wanted them to listen to the recordings of Hari's voice to gauge their reaction. His agent had been charmed and had agreed with Luc that the Hallelujah duet he had made with Hari should be included on the album. They could either disclose her real name or give her a pseudonym. Angie, for example! The shopping trip proved to be more of an exploratory expedition for Luc since Hari only bought a card and a silk scarf for her mother. She refused all gifts for herself, saying that Luc had already bought her enough. Having her parents to stay was present enough for her. Luc decided not to argue but to keep his own counsel.

While they were out, Luc took great care to hold Hari's hand, to occasionally lean in for a kiss, to put his arm around her shoulders. He wanted to make it perfectly clear to anyone who was interested that they were an item. He wanted nothing clandestine about this relationship.

At the restaurant, Luc deliberately chose a table on the terrace in full view of other diners. He held hands with Hari, shared food with her, wiped a speck of cream off her face— acting like a man in love. Though Luc thought to himself—'*I am not acting!*' A few people approached asking for his autograph which he declined regretfully saying that he was on a date with a very special lady and it would be disrespectful to her not to give her his undivided attention. He was sure they understood, he added charmingly.

Hari could not believe how well things had worked out. Luc made no secret of their relationship. On the contrary, he went out of his way to draw attention to themselves. Despite her initial nerves, Hari really enjoyed herself. It was like being on an actual date and Luc was such good company. He made her laugh, he listened to her and he actually cared about her. She was shocked to realise that she was in love with him. When had that happened? He had become such an integral part of her life that she took it for granted that he would always be there. Dangerous thinking! Luc didn't want a permanent relationship; he had made that quite clear. So, where did that leave her? Could she carry on pretending? Hari realised that no matter what, she was committed to Luc. If he wanted to set boundaries to their relationship, then she would accept it as long as they were together. But, what if he met someone and fell in love? What a thoroughly disturbing thought! Well, then she would have to resign her job and move on. All these tortured thoughts were racing through her mind and they must have shown on her face as Luc bent towards her saying:

"Hari, mein Liebchen, what are you thinking? You suddenly looked quite fierce and then sad? What is it, Schätzi?"

"Oh, nothing really. I was just enjoying our day together so much and hoping it could be like this forever. Then I realised that happiness like this doesn't last and I felt sad. Just ignore me, Cariad. I don't know what has gotten into me!"

"It is understandable that your emotions are on a rollercoaster considering what you have been through. But, I am glad to hear that you are enjoying today. Me too! I can't remember a time when I have felt so relaxed. I am sad to hear you say this happiness can't last though, Hari! Why must it end?"

"Oh, don't mind me! I am being silly! Let's change the subject before I spoil the day," she suggested.

Luc did as she asked but was left with an uneasy feeling. What did she mean? Was she perhaps getting tired of him? Oh, he hoped not! She had come to mean so much to him. Suddenly, Luc felt unsure of himself and felt a slight feeling of panic. He had assumed that Hari felt the same way about him. What if he were wrong? It took a huge effort for them both to regain some of their earlier joy which was now underlined by a slight feeling of unease. He had hoped that

178

such a public show of affection would convince Hari of his feelings for her.

Chapter Twenty-One

Working through Luc's diary the next day, Hari was excited to report three new invitations. Luc had been asked to perform in Vienna in June for the Midsummer concert at the Schönbrunn Palace. In July, there was the final André Rieu concert in Maastricht. In December, André Rieu would also be performing at the Royal Albert Hall in London and invited Luc to perform with him again. Hari was delighted when Luc accepted all three invitations. But, first they had the Paris trip to look forward to next month, plus a visit by her parents. The diary was filling up nicely. Luc had almost finished recording his duets album and was hoping to debut some of the songs in Paris.

In the meantime, Hari was looking forward to introducing Luc to the Six Nations Rugby Union Tournament, always a must-see event in the Price/Morgan households. She didn't know how popular it was in Switzerland as that country did not participate but she was sure it would be televised somewhere. She had asked her mother to post her favourite Welsh rugby shirt in time for the start of the tournament convinced that it brought luck to the national side when she wore it! It was a true revelation to Luc seeing the normally well-behaved Hari become quite agitated and shouting at the screen as she cheered on her team. As soon as she donned that jersey, she became welsher than Welsh! She sang along to the national anthem, roared at the forwards to score tries and screamed at the defence to block the opposition. When her team won, she was delirious, when they lost she was inconsolable. It was a truly exhausting experience and Luc enjoyed every minute of it. Who knew there was a hidden dragon within this tiny Welsh woman? He loved her passionate enjoyment for what was a national sport and he marvelled at the sheer exuberance of the Welsh voices as they sang their support for the players. With relations between her families restored, she had long phone calls home reliving the matches and sharing their joy and despair.

Watching the tournament, Luc realised how important music and singing were to the Welsh. It was an integral part of their makeup. Their national anthem was sung with such harmony and fervour that it resonated in his soul. When he heard the Welsh spectators singing *Calon lan,* he thought he had never heard anything so beautiful. He would get Hari to sing it to him later.

Luc had never felt such tension as the final between England and Wales—the old combatants. It was suddenly important to him for Wales to win as it meant so much to Hari. He found himself cheering them on and getting quite as vocal as her. He had never really watched sport before but this was exceptional. Maybe they could get tickets next year and watch it live in Cardiff? The match was close but Wales scored a last-minute try to take the victory. Hari's joy was unbelievable—she hurled herself at Luc knocking him over in the process. With their personal celebration which followed,

Luc was only too glad that they were not watching the match live or they would have been arrested!

Chapter Twenty-Two

March saw the arrival of Hari's parents in Gstaad. Luc drove Hari to the airport to meet them. He held back while Hari rushed to greet them as they came through the arrivals gate. Talking excitedly, with a huge smile on her face, she pulled them towards him.

"Mam, Dad, this is Luc!" she said, grabbing hold of his hand, as if she would never let him go.

With his free hand, Luc shook hands with the Prices saying how pleased he was to finally meet them. He hoped they would have a lovely visit and that they should stay as long as they liked.

"Oh, thank you, bach! It really is most kind of you to put us up like this," Cerys Price gushed, clearly captivated by his good looks and his charming manner. She gave her daughter a look to convey her appreciation.

"Not at all! It is my pleasure! Hari has been told she must not think about working while you are here—I know she has lots planned."

Mr and Mrs Price were stunned and not a little overawed by Luc's impressive home. He made it quite clear that they were to make themselves completely at home. When Hari showed her parents up to their room, they expressed their amazement at Luc and his home.

"Duw, but he is a lovely man!" said her mother, quite starry-eyed. "What a house, Cariad! You have landed on your feet here, love!"

"I know, Mam. Luc is a true gentleman and the best boss I have ever had. I am so lucky to have found this job. It is amazing. I get to travel all over with him. And the clothes I get to wear. I feel like Cinderella."

"Well, he is certainly good looking enough to be your prince," asserted Cerys Price.

"Now then, ladies, let's not get carried away," interjected Mr Price. "Looks aren't everything, you know! But, he does seem to be nice, Cariad," he said to Hari. "I shall reserve judgement until I get to know him a little better of course."

"Aw, Dad, he is truly lovely. There is no side to him. What you see is what you get! I know you will like him. Now then let me show you around the house—I hope you have bought your swimming togs like I said—wait till you see the pool!"

The Prices visit went exceedingly well. Despite Luc saying that Hari should take the time off, she organised it so that she spent a few hours each day sorting through the mail and updating the calendar, ensuring that Luc was made aware of all changes. While Luc worked in his recording studio, she then entertained her parents, taking them out on outings. In the evenings, they ate together, delicious meals which Hari insisted on cooking, often helped by Luc.

It was overall a relaxed visit once Hari's parents have got over their initial shyness. Luc was charm personified and really enjoyed having visitors. On Cerys' birthday, he booked a meal out for them all. She was delighted with her silk scarf from Hari and Luc had bought her a leather bag which Hari ensured him her mother would love. Cerys accepted it gratefully, thought protesting that he had already done so much, paying for their fares and putting them up.

"It is my pleasure, Cerys," Luc assured her. "I am just glad that you like it. Now, we must have a bottle of champagne to celebrate your birthday. I know Hari is particularly partial to a glass of bubbly!" he quipped.

Hari's parents were amazed at how easy Luc was to talk to. He was far more famous than they realised going by the attention he drew wherever he went. Yet, he was charming and friendly, quite unlike the unfair portrayal of him in the newspaper article. They realised that there was more to Hari's relationship with her boss than just a working one—but they were very discreet about things so no offence could be taken. It was obvious from their body language that they cared for each other. Despite their ill feelings about the marriage break-up, they were nevertheless relieved to see that Hari was being so well looked after and happy. Happier than they had seen her in years! Maybe marriage to Rhodri had not been right, after all? Like all parents they just wanted her to be happy and cherished—it seemed that Luc was able to do just that, so he had their blessing.

Saying farewell to her parents at the airport, Hari became quite tearful. The visit went better than she could have imagined with her relationship with her parents restored to what it had always been. She was delighted how well Luc got on with them and she was sure that they liked him, too. She was pretty convinced that they realised her relationship with Luc was not just a business one as she had caught her mother's significant glances on more than one occasion. But, she felt that they approved, despite her still being legally married.

Waving them off, Luc took hold of Hari's hand and squeezed it gently, understanding her emotions. He was glad that the visit went well and that Hari was back on good terms with her parents since he knew how much of a family person she was. He was also pleased to have been given their blessing when Mr Price took him aside and told him exactly that!

"Well, Schätzi! That went well, I think. I like your parents. I can see where you get your fiery temper from now," he quipped.

"I don't know what you mean!" she quickly replied. "I don't have a temper—well not much of one, anyway."

"Of course not, Liebchen. It is all in my imagination!" he replied with a grin. "Now, let us go home and have some quality time together. I have been dying to get you alone for the last two weeks."

"Oh, Luc! You know we spent time together—don't exaggerate!"

"Yes, but we had to be so quiet! Not that it wasn't fun seducing you quietly. You are usually such a noisy lover!"

Hari thumped him playfully on the arm, "Oh, you! What a thing to say!"

"But you know it is the truth!" he replied innocently. "Let's get home quickly and I shall prove it to you! Good job my house is soundproofed or else the police will think someone is being murdered."

Although Hari had loved seeing her parents, she was delighted to get back to their routine. Luc had been the most charming host but had reined in some of their more intimate actions, which she greatly missed. He would nuzzle her neck in passing, kiss her hair, whisper sweet nothings in her ear, kiss her spontaneously whenever near her and often pull her into an embrace or even a waltz. Likewise, she loved to come up behind him and just wrap her arms around him, resting her head against his back. When watching television or reading together, she loved to stretch out on the sofa with her head in his lap with Luc absent-mindedly stroking her hair.

She was totally, deeply in love with him and was pretty sure that he must feel the same. But he could not say anything while she was still married. He would not want to put any pressure on her.

Then out of the blue, she received an urgent phone call from Rhodri begging her to meet with him. He would fly to Gstaad and meet wherever she suggested but he needed to talk to her urgently. He refused to discuss the matter over the phone saying it was something that had to be said face to face. So, Hari set up a meeting for the next afternoon, not letting Luc know about the call or the meeting. She did not want to worry him but was feeling extremely anxious herself.

Luc, of course, knew something was troubling Hari. She had such an open face that she could not hide anything from him. But he trusted her to tell him what was wrong in her own time. He was not surprised when Hari casually mentioned that she had an errand to run the next day and did he want anything while she was out. He decided he would take the opportunity of her being busy to buy her birthday present. But, Luc was stunned when exiting the jewellery shop that afternoon to see Hari sitting in the window of the cafe opposite—she was with her husband! He was holding her hands across the table and it looked such an intimate scene that it unnerved him somewhat. Now he was in a dilemma. Should he pretend not to see them and go home or should he keep an eye on her in case she needed him?

He was even more concerned when Hari started to cry and Rhodri stood up to cuddle her. She let him! What was happening? Surely, they were not getting back together? Luc felt his heart was breaking. When Rhodri bent down and kissed Hari on the lips, he thought he would explode. No, she can't go back to him! She belonged here with him.

Rhodri was leaving! Without Hari? What should he do now? The decision was taken for him when Hari stumbled out of the cafe in obvious distress. Without hesitating, Luc rushed towards her and folded her in his arms with her whole body wracked with sobs. Trying to avoid concerned glances from passers-by Luc hurried her over to his car.

"Hari! Liebchen! Shh! It is alright, don't take on so, Schätzi! Ach, it breaks my heart to see you so upset. Shh! It is alright. I am here. I won't let anything bad happen to you."

His comforting words had no effect on a very distraught Hari. He was becoming seriously worried. All he could do was hug her and comfort her and hope that she would calm enough to talk to him. In her silence, he was fearing the worst!

"Hari, my love! Please tell me what is wrong! Why were you meeting with your husband? What did he say to you that has upset you so much? Please talk to me!"

Seeing that Hari was calming down, he handed her a hanky, making a joke, "Seems I am always giving you my hankies, Liebchen! Soon I will have none left!"

"I shall buy you some new ones," hiccupped a very upset Hari, slowly returning to her senses. "Oh, Luc, he wants a quick divorce!"

"But, that is wonderful news, Schätzi! Why does that upset you so?"

"Because he has only got his other woman pregnant!" she sobbed even louder.

"Oh, I am so sorry, Schätzi. That is so hurtful for you."

"He knows how much I wanted a baby. How could he do this to me! The bastard!" she muttered angrily. "All those years I was with him and nothing. He has a one-night stand in his own words and gets her pregnant. It is not fair!" she sobbed.

"I know, my love! But at least now you can get your divorce and move forward with your life," he said quietly. But, in her present mood this was no consolation to Hari.

"Come, my love. Let me drive us home. I can fetch your car later. You need time to process this news and this is not the right place to do that."

Hari nodded her consent. Leaning across her, Luc put on her seat belt and then drove them home glancing worriedly at her every now and again. He was so out of his depth on this one and wasn't sure how to behave towards her.

Back in the house, Hari curled up into a ball of misery and rocked herself silently. Luc kept a cautious eye on her but decided that he would leave her to thoughts. He instinctively felt that whatever he said now would be taken the wrong way. When he felt it was safe to leave her, Luc made his way to the kitchen and started preparing the evening meal. He wasn't sure that Hari would eat anything but he had to keep busy. He had never felt so out of his depth. He wished his mother was here but realised that it was not his problem to share.

Putting on some gentle, relaxing music, Luc worked quietly in the kitchen. He was so engrossed that he was taken completely by surprise when Hari arms encircled him and she rested her head against his back. Unable to see her face he patted her hands comfortingly.

"Hello, Liebchen! As you can see, I am cooking your favourite meal although you may not want to eat anything. I feel so useless but I had to do something."

"Thank you, Cariad," Hari replied in a small voice. "I am sorry I reacted so badly. It was such a shock. I have always wanted a baby, you see. It was a great sorrow that we never had one. I feel cheated in a strange way."

He asked gently, "I can see that, Liebchen. Do you know why you never conceived? Did you have tests?"

"No! It just never happened. Maybe I am sterile! Obviously Rhodri isn't," she said bitterly.

"Sshh, my love. Don't get upset again! Maybe you were not compatible! If you are worried we could arrange for you to have tests done."

"Not now, Luc. I am too angry and upset. I need to calm down and come to terms with this ultimate betrayal. Well, the irony is that he wants an immediate divorce so they can marry! He has kept me waiting for nearly a year and suddenly it's all steam ahead! Oooh, I am so angry!"

"Shall we go down to the gym so you can use the punch ball, Liebchen!" quipped Luc, actually drawing a snigger from Hari.

"If you can put a photo of Rhodri on it, I would be delighted!" she replied with venom.

Luc burst out laughing at her ferocity which had the desired effect on Hari who joined in his laughter. Turning round to face her, Luc cupped her face gently, looking deep into her eyes, he said, "There is nothing we can't face together, Liebchen. Together we are stronger, nicht wahr?"

Luc desperately wanted to promise Hari the longed-for baby. He wanted to pledge himself to her but he knew he would have to bide his time. She was not ready to hear this declaration when her emotions were still so raw. So, instead he could love her and make her laugh and keep her busy. He was glad they had the imminent Paris trip as it would take her mind off everything else. He would also ensure that she had the best birthday ever in one of the world's most romantic cities.

Chapter Twenty-Three

Paris was everything Hari had dreamed of. She was excited to actually see in the flesh the famous landmarks she had only ever seen pictures of. Luc had promised her that there would be time for some sightseeing during the trip. He was scheduled to give five consecutive nights of performances during their ten day stay.

The hotel was opulent in the extreme. Their suite was luxury itself. Hari had packed all her new gowns, one for each performance, her two tea dresses for dinner dates and the pants outfits for any unscheduled invitations. She also packed casual clothes for off duty days when they could sightsee. Virginie had been spot on in her estimation of what Hari would need.

The concerts were sublime! There was a plethora of international artists soloing or duetting. Luc or Sebastien as he was known on the circuit performed a duet with Luigi Marconi an Italian tenor. They were then joined by Kurt Winter a baritone to sing *Nessun Dorma*. Their beautiful harmonies caused shivers up and down Hari's spine. Then Luc was back for his solo performance. To her surprise and delight he debuted *The First Time Ever I saw your Face* from his new album. He seemed to sing it directly to her—the words resonating in her heart. She felt so touched by his beautiful voice that she held her breath, gentle tears filling her eyes at the message he was so obviously sending her. She felt completely overwhelmed and was further astonished when he blew her a kiss at the end of the song before taking a bow to the audience. He was greeted with rapturous applause which boded well for his new album.

All acts returned to the stage for the finale and were forced to take several curtain calls so loud was the applause. Finally, the curtains remained drawn and the auditorium started to clear, the audience talking excitedly about the performance they had just had the privilege to witness.

Still stunned from this exceptional night of music, Hari remained in her seat until the coast was clear. Then she slowly made her way backstage to Luc's dressing room. As she knocked at the door, it was suddenly opened by Luc who pulled her into the room and into his arms kicking the door shut behind her.

"Well, what did you think? Did you like it?"

"I loved it! It felt like you were singing it just for me!"

"I was, couldn't you tell?" He replied. "I think the audience liked it. I am hopeful that the new album will be a hit. Komm, mein Liebchen, let's go back to the hotel. I am in need of a massage and some loving attention. I feel quite exhausted."

"Not too exhausted, I hope?" She queried.

"Well, you will just have to work on me, Schätzi!" he replied huskily, before kissing her long and hungrily, leaving her in no doubt that he was not too tired to play.

The subsequent performances were equally well received and Hari felt she would never tire of hearing Luc singing. His voice was so smooth like liquid silk and it never failed to move her. Each time he sang the song, it felt like the first time. The applause at the end of the final concert was even more rapturous than on the preceding evening. The whole concert had been a hit and would no doubt be repeated at a later date.

After that final concert, Luc and Hari took a day off and did some well-earned sightseeing. Luc had planned a full day of visiting as many of the famous monuments as was feasible. They climbed the Eiffel Tower; they walked along the Champs Elysées to the Arc de Triomphe and finally visited the Louvre so that Hari could see the famous Mona Lisa. Although she appreciated this iconic painting, she fell in love with the Madonna of the Rocks which hung alongside. She was so captivated by the vast number of famous canvasses that Luc bought her a book to commemorate their visit. It would also give her time to look at them in more detail and at her leisure since the museum was so vast it could not be completed in an afternoon!

The following day saw another engagement in the diary. They were to attend a garden party in the famous Tuileries gardens. Hari wore one of lovely tea dresses, a floral chiffon in shades of pink, nicely accentuating her auburn hair which she wore in a loose chignon. Cream platform wedges gave her added height and confidence. Luc thought she looked beautiful and he was proud to have her on his arm.

They wandered hand in hand around the beautiful gardens enjoying the early spring sunshine and revelling in each other's company. When Luc was called away by some acquaintances to discuss a business matter, Hari decided to fetch some food. She was biting into a delicate sandwich when a loud Italian voice caught her attention.

"Well, what do you have to say for yourself, Mrs Morgan? Are you not ashamed to be flaunting yourself with Sebastien? What does your husband think of all this? Have you no shame? Do you not care about Sebastien's reputation?" It was Maria Benedetto and she was making no effort to lower her voice.

On the contrary, she seemed determined to draw attention towards Hari. "I am sorry, but I am not answerable to you!" replied Hari trying to move away.

Maria angrily grabbed at her arm continuing to shout abuse at her, not caring who heard her accusations.

"If you cannot behave in a civilised fashion, I shall have no option but to do likewise. Let go of my arm and leave me in peace," warned Hari.

"Why, you strumpet! How dare you talk to me like that! Do you know who I am?" She shouted.

"Oh I am perfectly aware of you and your reputation. Now, kindly release my arm and get out of my way."

"Don't you dare walk away from me," screamed the Italian woman in an absolute rage.

"Sorry, but you asked for this!" muttered Hari, throwing her wine at Maria. It splashed all over her face and spilled down the front of her dress, causing her to roar in outrage. She was just about to hurl herself at Hari when Luc appeared and placed himself between the two ladies.

"So, Maria, I see you are making quite a spectacle of yourself. I think you should go and calm down, my dear. You might like to clean up a little too."

"Did you see what that little hussy did?" She screamed.

"I believe she had provocation. I heard her quite clearly give you fair warning. Come now, Maria. You have to be able to take abuse if you are going to give it!"

"Why she is an adulteress! What do you see in her anyway?"

"Be very careful what you say, Maria. Say anything more derogatory and I might forget I am a gentleman," he warned.

"Come, Schätzi! There is someone I would like to introduce you to," he said smiling at her.

Taking Hari by the hand, he led her away greeting people as if nothing had happened. She admired his self-control and sheer presence! But he had not been called an adulteress and had his private life bandied about so openly. She breathed deeply to try and slow her racing heartbeat. Luc gently squeezed her hand to show he understood how she was feeling. He bent to whisper in her ear, "Smile! Laugh as if I had just said something incredibly witty!" he grinned at her. "Don't show how upset you are, mein Liebchen," he added kissing her gently on the cheek.

Following his advice, Hari laughed aloud. He squeezed her hand again as if to say well done! She allowed herself to relax when she realised that people were not judging her poor behaviour. On the contrary, they seemed intrigued to meet the feisty lady who had taken on a temperamental Italian diva and won! Curious to know her better, they knew not to ask any personal questions with Luc in attendance. So, they made polite conversations. She would never remember all the people she was introduced to, but that didn't matter. She just had to smile and be charming as Luc was adept at small talk.

After what seemed like hours, they took their leave and returned to their hotel. Hari started to apologise for embarrassing him but he interrupted her, "You have nothing to apologise for! I am sorry that you were subjected to the bad behaviour of a jealous woman. Maria cannot accept that there will never be anything between us and it is making her spiteful and unpleasant. That is not your fault, Schätzi! Please try to forget about it. Now, I am feeling rather tense after all that excitement—how about a massage and a bath?" He winked suggestively at her.

She asked with a grin, "Is that for me or for you?"

"I thought it could be mutually rewarding! You scratch my back and I will scratch yours!"

"Ah, but my nails are longer!" she purred.

"I know and I can hardly wait!" he growled in anticipation, pulling her into his arms and tickling her until she screamed for him to stop.

"Ok, pax!" he said, finally releasing her. "Why don't you run the bath—make it deep and bubbly! I will fetch up some drinks and meet you in there!"

She asked innocently, "Oh, are you going to help me undress?"

"No, because if I do, we shall never make it to the bath!" he threatened. Giggling Hari made her way slowly to the bathroom taking off one item of clothing at a time and dropping it on the floor. Luc watched her in amusement— what a little minx! He was determined not to rush his planned seduction, wanting to take all evening if necessary.

Chapter Twenty-Four

Hari woke the next morning to a room full of flowers—daffodils! Wherever had he got these? In the middle of the room was a large silver balloon inscribed with Happy Birthday. On the bed itself was a small package and a card. Luc was rudely awakened when Hari leapt on him and started kissing him.

"Did I not tire you out last night, Liebchen?" He mumbled against her lips, his eyes smiling in amusement.

"Oh, Cariad, thank you!"

"It was my pleasure," he replied. "But you thanked me last night, you know, several times if I remember!"

"Oh, you! No, you remembered!"

"Why of course, I remembered. It was a memorable night after all! Oh, look at all these flowers," he teased. "Is it someone's birthday?"

"Stop teasing, Cariad! Thank you! What a lovely surprise! I didn't even realise that you knew when my birthday was."

"Well, aren't you going to open your present? Oh, there are some more cards here, too!" he added, reaching under his side of the bed and bringing out a stack of cards and presents.

"Oh, I wondered why mam hadn't sent anything. Not like her at all!"

"Open these first, Liebchen!" said Luc, pushing her family's presents forward.

Hari opened the cards first. She was surprised to find a card and a letter of apology from Rhodri's parents. She put the letter aside not wanting to spoil the happiness which was bubbling inside her. For the same reason, she wouldn't open the card from Rhodri. He had no right to impinge on her special time with Luc and she wasn't sure she wanted to read anything from him anyway. She was still angry with him and extremely hurt. Luc noticed her actions but decided not to comment. Today was supposed to be about Hari and making her happy. He realised how much joy it gave him seeing her happy.

When Hari got to the final card which was from Luc, she found a loving message alongside some cryptic clues. When she looked at him with raised eyebrows he simply said, "Solve the clues for more treats! But, the first one comes free," he added pushing the package towards her.

A little bemused by this secrecy, Hari opened Luc's first present. It was heart shaped gold locket and chain.

"Oh, Luc, Cariad, I absolutely love it! Thank you so much!" she said reaching over to kiss him.

"I am glad you like it! It has a special meaning which will become clear if you solve your clues," he replied enigmatically. "Here, let me help you. Now if you look in the box you should find your first clue!"

Hari found a folded card in the bottom of the box. When she opened it up, the message read, go to the place where the artists are and ask for Jean-Luc! "What on earth can that mean?" She pondered.

"Artists?" Presumably not an art gallery if I am seeking someone called Jean-Luc. So, how about a local artist?

"What is the name of the famous place where you can get your portrait done? Up near that lovely church on the hill?"

"Do you mean the Sacré Cœur? The Montmartre district?" Luc replied giving nothing away from his expression.

"Yes, that's the one! Is that where I am supposed to go? Oh, come on, Luc, you will have to help me a little bit. I don't know Paris after all."

"Ok, point taken. Yes that is the right answer," he replied with a smile looking at her serious face. This was supposed to be enjoyable, so he had better be ready to help if he didn't want to spoil her surprises.

"Right, come on, let's get over to Montmartre so you can look for Jean-Luc," he suggested.

When they arrived at Montmartre, Hari was overwhelmed by the sheer number of artists in the square. How on earth was she supposed to find one particular man? Then she noticed a daffodil sitting atop an easel and gave Luc a huge grin. How typical of him?

As she approached, she noticed a painter doing a portrait of a tourist. She stood and watched in fascination until he finished. Then she asked him if his name was Jean-Luc.

"Mais, oui, Mademoiselle, Alors, asseyez-vous, s'il vous plaît!"

He proceeded to sketch her portrait quickly and with great dexterity. When he handed the completed sketch to Hari, she was astonished at the likeness.

"Oh, merci, Monsieur. C'est formidable!" she thanked him.

"De rien, Mademoiselle. Bon Anniversaire!" he said and handed over his card as he wished her farewell.

"Oh, Luc, thank you! That's so lovely. I shall never forget this—it isn't everyday a girl has her portrait done!"

"I am glad you like it, Liebchen. Maybe you should look more closely at the card," he hinted.

Turning it over, Hari saw another clue.

High on a hill is a sacred building which holds a secret!

"Oh, that must mean the Sacré Cœur! Come on, Luc," she said, pulling him by the hand. This time she didn't need any help with the clue.

Perched at the top of some steep steps was the most beautiful church painted in gleaming white—it certainly stood out. Hari pulled Luc right to the top where she had to pause to catch her breath. The views over Paris were sublime. But she didn't feel she had time to waste and headed towards the entrance. In the porch was a solitary daffodil! Hurrying inside, Hari wondered what her surprise was this time. She was greeted with the sound of an organ starting up and suddenly a choir appeared in front of the altar and started to sing. Hari sat down in the nearest pew and grabbed hold of Luc's hand. They were singing for her! They sang *Make you feel my Love* and *Stand by Me*, both songs which she knew Luc had included on his duets album. This was so magical! She could hardly breathe—their voices harmonised beautifully.

At the end, she clasped her hands together and mouthed, "Merci!" as the choir members exited towards the back of the altar. Only the choirmaster remained and walking towards her he handed her a card saying, "Bon Anniversaire, Mademoiselle!"

Hari felt her heart would burst from happiness. What a special birthday this was turning out to be. She didn't know if she could stand any more surprises. Still she opened the card and read: *His master's voice! Go where he received his training!*

"That means you, Luc, isn't it? Didn't you say that you studied at the conservatoire here in Paris?" She asked.

At his nod, she added, "Well, I guess that is our next stop. Oh, Luc, thank you so much. I don't know how you managed to arrange all this."

"It's my absolute pleasure, Liebchen! Come on, we have more surprises to go! Can't keep them waiting!" he smiled enigmatically, pulling her by the hand.

Pinned to the door handle of the celebrated Conservatoire de Musique was a bright yellow daffodil. Pushing open the huge double doors, Luc led the way towards an auditorium. Opening the doors, he pushed Hari ahead of him. In the centre of the room was a small orchestra with two singers standing to one side. Luc gestured Hari to a seat as the orchestra began to play. There followed a performance of four more of Luc's duets. Once again, the singing was sublime and sounded even better when supported by this wonderfully talented orchestra. Hari was transported into a dream like state. She applauded enthusiastically at the end and thanked them many times over. One of the singers approached and wished her a happy birthday, while handing over a card and a small package.

"Oh, Luc, surely not more! I don't want to appear ungrateful, but I don't think I can take much more excitement."

"You would be surprised, Schätzi! Go on, open it!"

The small package held a CD of Sebastien's new album Duets! It was signed and dedicated to Hari.

"Hot off the press, Liebchen! This is the very first copy!" he explained with a smile at her awed expression. Tears of joy were filling her eyes, so he took out his handkerchief and gently wiped her face. Kissing her softly on the lips he said, "Right, let us look at the next clue. I must say whoever thought this up is a very clever fellow!" which brought forth a guffaw from Hari and a punch on his arm.

Quasimodo's lady friend has a significance for the next gift!

"What? Quasimodo is from Victor Hugo's book. It was based around Notre Dame. Wasn't the lady called Esmeralda? Well, I guess that means we are off to Notre Dame."

Luc nodded his confirmation and led the way. Sure enough the tell-tale daffodil greeted their arrival. But this time, they were not greeted by any music. Instead there was a message on the notice board addressed to Angarad Morgan with a drawing of a daffodil on it. Hari pulled it down and read the clue:

Find the organ player and mention Esmeralda!

Puzzled Hari walked into the cathedral looking for the organ. She heard music emanating from one of the naves— that must be the organ! Heading towards the sound she was pleased to see a man playing the organ. She approached quietly not wanting to interrupt his playing, but waiting patiently until the end of the song. Sure enough as the last note died away, the man turned towards her with an expectant smile. Hari smiled back and said, "Bonjour, Monsieur. Je cherche Esmeralda."

"Bonjour, Mademoiselle, et bon Anniversaire!" Reaching to the side of the organ, he fetched out a little package and a card which he handed to Hari with a smile.

"Merci, Monsieur!" Returning to Luc's side, Hari opened the small package and was astounded to find some emerald ear-rings with a little note saying emeralds for my Esmeralda—with her beautiful green eyes!

"Oh, Luc! They are so beautiful!" she whispered awe-struck! "Oh, this is too much! You are far too generous!"

"Right, I shall take them back then, shall I?" He quipped reaching over to take the box.

"Certainly not! I absolutely love them!" she replied.

"That's a relief," he quipped. "They took some finding, you know. They had to be the exact shade of green. I nearly drove the jeweller demented as I rejected so many! Come on, put them on! I need to see if I got the colour right!" Hari obliged and Luc was delighted with the result. They were a perfect match for her shining eyes. Seeing that she was getting over emotional and obviously tired from all their traipsing around, Luc suggested that they have a refreshment stop before she opened the next clue.

On reaching the restaurant of Luc's choice, Hari looked around suspiciously for any sign of daffodils. No obvious sign, she thought with some relief. Now she could enjoy a respite!

She asked timidly, "I am not being ungrateful, Cariad, but are there many more clues?"

"I have saved the best till last, I hope," he replied. "Back at the hotel! So you can relax and enjoy your food. So, birthday girl, what will you have? Want to try some oysters? I believe they are an aphrodisiac!" he said innocently. "Not that you need one!" he added quickly at her outraged expression.

"No thanks, I will stick to something safe. I don't know if oysters would agree with me. Best to play safe!"

They ordered a leisurely meal taking their time over each course. When they finished, Luc ordered a taxi to take them back to their hotel as he could see that Hari was tired.

Chapter Twenty-Five

Back at the hotel, Luc followed Hari into their suite. She stood inside the door and looked around. She didn't know what she was looking for, as there were so many daffodils, which one was hiding a clue? She looked towards Luc for a hint and he jerked his head towards the bed.

Why hadn't she seen that? Because she was looking for a daffodil and not the heart-shaped box of chocolates that rested on the pillows. Picking it up, she took off the bow-covered lid and saw rows of heart-shaped chocolates. Selecting one, she popped it in her mouth—delicious! She selected another and offered it to Luc. Then she looked in the box for a clue. There it was under the bottom layer.

You have stolen my heart!

A simple message with a clear meaning but where did it lead? She looked around the room this time not focussing on the daffodils and she noticed a small teddy bear holding a heart! That must be the next clue!

Picking up the bear, she noticed it was sitting on a large envelope. When she opened it, she was surprised to see a contract of employment which had been crossed out. The accompanying sheet had the words, 'You are Fired!' At the bottom of the sheet was a drawing of a diamond solitaire with an IOU label attached. There was an arrow indicating that she should turn over the page. On the back was a drawing of her iPod with the words Play Me!

"What on earth! Luc, you are firing me!" she said outraged and upset. "I can't believe it!"

"Wait, Hari! Follow all the instructions," he interrupted her hoping this was not going to go horribly wrong.

Completely mystified and somewhat indignant, Hari glared at Luc and then went to follow the instructions. She sat on the bed a little deflated and refused to lean into him when he sat beside her. Then the music started and she was mesmerised. It was Luc's voice singing an unknown song! As she listened to the words, she realised that he was singing to her and her alone. It was the most beautiful love song. Surely, he hadn't written it? She gradually relaxed against him as he enfolded her in his arms. She wasn't sure where this was going but that song was magical.

"Did you write that?" She asked in amazement when the song ended.

"Guilty!" whispered Luc into her ear. "Just for you, my love! To tell you how I feel."

"But you just sacked me!"

"Ah, but there is more to it than that! Look for clues!"

Hari gazed around the room, perplexed. She got up and walked around. As she circled the room, she noticed something stuck to the back of the balloon. It was an envelope! Carefully prising it off, she opened it up to find two more sheets of paper. The first was a sketch of a man on bended knee proposing to a red-headed woman—herself and Luc? The second sheet was a facsimile of a marriage contract.

Hari looked up in shock to find Luc on bended knee in front of her.

Taking her gently by the hand he said, "I have ripped up that ridiculous contract because I want something more permanent. I love you so much, my little Welsh wonder, that I would be very honoured if you would agree to become my wife. It can be a long engagement as long as the answer is yes. Well, say something, Hari! I don't think I can stand the suspense much longer."

Hari felt her eyes filling with tears. So, that was what all this was about! How did she feel about marriage? She was technically still married to Rhodri. Could she go through it all again? With the right man, yes! She knew that Luc was a very different proposition to Rhodri. She could trust him not to cheat, he was too honest. But, did she want marriage? She knew that he had become an integral part of her life is such a short time. If she was honest, she could not imagine him not being part of her life. Why did things have to change? Wasn't he happy with their present arrangement? Realising that he was still waiting for her answer and looking very unsure of himself she decided to speak:

"Luc, I love you too! I think I loved you from the first moment we met and it has been growing steadily. But I am still married. I am not sure if I am ready to commit to something so permanent yet. What about my job? I love it! I am not sure I could stand it if you had another assistant who travelled everywhere with you. Where would I be?"

"First, my love, I am relieved to hear that you love me, too. I was getting worried there. I want to let you know how I feel about you and what my intentions are long term. I want you both as my wife and my business partner. I want you by the side on a permanent basis. I know it is far too soon to be talking about marriage which is why I am suggesting a long engagement. But I would really like that commitment, Liebchen. To show you how very much I love you and need you. I want to shout it to the world that I am in love with this beautiful, amazing lady. It can be a secret between ourselves until such time as you feel comfortable announcing it to the world. But could you please give me some hope? Have I got this terribly wrong?"

"Oh, Luc! All I can promise you at the moment is that I love you with my whole heart and that I can't imagine being apart from you. If that means marriage, then my answer is yes! But please let me carry on as your assistant as I love my job!" she added.

"But of course, you must keep your job—who else is going to protect me from all those crazy fans and prima donnas who will insist on throwing themselves at me! I need my little Welsh dragon of a bodyguard! I can't imagine you not being right there beside me, either. These last few months have been the happiest of my life and I thank the day I followed my conscience and went back to rescue my little novice skier. You have literally changed my life—for the better. I can't wait to tell Maman and Vati—though I think they will not be surprised!"

So saying, he swept her into his arms and carried her over to the bed. "And now, Liebchen, I have one more birthday present for you," he murmured, nuzzling her neck.

"Aw, Luc, you saved the best till last!" smiled Hari, returning his kisses with an ardour to match his own.

THE END